Easy Ride

A Military/Curvy Girl MC Romance

Nichole Rose

Nichole Rose

Contents

Dedication

To J – Your HEA is coming, beautiful.

About the Book

Loving his curvy lamb will be this former SEAL's easiest ride yet.

Shep

Ainsley Foster has the brightest eyes and sweetest smile I've ever seen.

Whatever she's running from sent her straight to my gym.

I want her to run right into my arms.

But earning her trust is no easy feat.

All she knows of motorcycle clubs is what she's seen on the news.

She knows nothing of men like me—those willing to die to protect the people they love.

No matter, though.

Teaching this sweet lamb will be the easiest ride of my life.

Ainsley

Shep Stratford is the strongest man I've ever met.

He's ex-military. Quiet. Ridiculously strong. Wickedly hot.

He's also in a motorcycle club.

Yet, when I'm anywhere near him, all I feel is safe.

He knows I'm running from something. He says it doesn't matter.

But he doesn't know the biggest billionaire in Wyoming is looking for me.

When he finds out the truth, will he still want to keep me?

Or will my uncle's money ruin the best thing in my life?

Warning When this former SEAL meets his little lamb, he'll do whatever it takes to teach her that she belongs with him. If you enjoy growly alphas, adorable heroines, and safe MC romance that's light on drama, you'll love Shep and Ainsley. This sweet, steamy romance from Nichole Rose comes complete with a sticky sweet and guaranteed HEA.

Chapter One

"Excuse me."

I glance up from my booth at Rooster's, searching for the woman speaking. For a minute, I think she's talking to me, but I'm completely alone in my corner, my back to the wall like usual. Public places and I don't mesh well. Luckily, Rooster's is owned by Logan McCray, another member of the Men of Valor, our MC. Trouble doesn't blow through the doors without blowing right back out again.

Valor, Wyoming has seen its fair share of problems lately though. That's what happens when the men who are supposed to do the protecting are the same ones the town needs protecting from. The cops here are as dirty as they come. My Brothers and I don't stand for it. Dirty cops tend not to like it when the local motorcycle club gets all up in their business. But hey, the trash won't take itself out.

And we've taken out a lot of trash lately. The Chief of Police is gone. So are the bastards who worked with him. I still don't trust the rest of them.

Neither do most of my Brothers. The majority of us are ex-military.

Let's just say none of us have a particular liking for men who abuse their power or fail to protect their flock. Keeping people safe is who we are and what we know. Most of us are out of the service now, but it's in our blood. We do what we can to clean up the town and handle what needs handled.

Rooster and his ol' lady keep this place clean, and since I'm shit at making coffee, the corner booth and I are well acquainted. Coffee is my vise, and pie is my guilty pleasure. I eat the hell out of it. I own the local gym and spend most of my time training, so I figure it balances in the grand scheme of things. And if not...fuck it. A man has needs. And I need pie.

Like I said, it balances.

"What can I do for you?" Rooster says, calling my attention to the long counter.

As soon as I set eyes on the woman standing there, my heart starts pounding. My cock does too. She's maybe five-three, barely tall enough to see over the counter without the fuck-me heels on her feet. She's thick and curvy, filling out her blue vintage dress in ways that ought to be illegal. Her curly black hair is pinned back from her round face in a handkerchief that matches the dress, leaving the diamonds in her ears visible. She's gorgeous...and nervous as hell.

She's practically squirming where she stands, her hands fisted into the sides of her dress like it's the only way to keep them still. They're clenched so tight, her knuckles are white. I don't know who she is but she's a shy little thing. Sweet. Exactly the kind of girl the cops around here love to target.

I've never seen her around before now. Which means she's new here. Knowing things is what I do. I spent fifteen years working intelligence as a SEAL. I was the guy they sent in when they needed boots on the ground to get intel. Not much happens around here that I don't know. Old habits die hard and all that shit.

"Um, I was wondering if you were hiring?" she asks Rooster. Her voice is soft, dulcet.

My dick hasn't gotten hard for anything in years, but he's certainly standing at attention now. Fuck me. Those curves are sweeter than the pie I love so much. I can just imagine how soft she'll be when I'm gripping her hips and pounding into her from behind, that musical voice moaning my name into the room.

"You looking for a job?" Rooster asks.

I don't even have to look at him to know he shares my surprise. Rooster pays well and we all leave big tips for the staff, but the diamonds in her ears are probably worth more than she'd make here in six months. The red bottoms on her heels and the cut of her dress make it obvious they both sport designer labels.

There's only one reason a girl like her blows into a town like Valor. She's running...either to something or away from something. I quickly check her finger, but don't see a ring. No lines either. She isn't married. Shit. I'm not even sure if she's old enough to be married. She's young.

Which should be all the reason I need to keep my ass in the booth where I'm at, but I don't. Of-fucking-course I don't. My Brothers give me shit for it, but I've got a soft spot for strays. I grew up without family, so I know a thing or two about being alone in the world. It isn't fun.

I've brought more than a few strays home to the club over the years.

Never wanted to fuck one before now. That's new. So is the emotion bubbling up from some pit deep in my stomach. The thought of this girl taking on the world by herself sends anxiety churning through me. She's too sweet, too innocent. Some good-for-nothing SOB will be all over her before she even knows what's happening.

That's not going to work for me. I don't want anyone touching her. Except for me. And I want to put my hands all over her.

If she's not eighteen, my big ass will be going to church, pronto. And I don't mean the one in the back of the club. I'm talking sitting in a confessional, praying for forgiveness to avoid fire and brimstone. That kind of church. Because there is nothing holy about the things I want to do to this girl.

"Yes," she says to Rooster, her chin coming up like she expects a fight. "I heard you might be hiring. Are you?"

Rooster sees me headed their way out of the corner of his eye. His gaze shifts in my direction.

I quickly shake my head, telling him no.

He catches what I'm throwing.

"Not at the moment," he tells her.

Her shoulders droop.

I don't like that much. Makes my guts burn like I've got a blade in them.

"I'm hiring."

She jerks, her hand flying to her heart like I scared her. She turns in my direction, and my heart lodges itself in my throat. I've never seen eyes as bright as hers. They're sky blue and shining with moisture.

Is she crying? Shit.

I shove my hands into my pockets, trying to keep myself from reaching out to pull her into my arms to comfort her. It's been...shit, I was going to say it's been a hot minute since I last held a woman to comfort her, except I can't remember ever holding a woman to comfort her. But I want to do it with this one. She looks so damn small and sad.

The vulnerability in her gaze is striking.

I don't think she's running to anything. More like running from it and running hard.

The thought has my protective instincts soaring. At thirty-eight, I learned long ago to listen to my gut. It's saved my ass on more than one occasion. I'm not sure exactly what it's trying to tell me right now, but I know I'm not letting this girl leave without tying her to me in some way.

"You're hiring?" Her wide eyes eat me alive, and I can tell by the pink staining her cheeks that she likes what she sees.

Owning a gym has its perks. I'm a big son of a bitch from head to toe. At six-three, I loom over her, but she doesn't seem nervous. Which is a strong indication that whoever she's running from didn't hurt her. That's a good thing. Because I don't even know her name yet, but I already know killing to avenge her wouldn't bother me at all.

"Yeah." I clear my throat. "I own a gym."

"Stratford Training and Fitness?"

"You know it?" I ask, surprised. Either she's been here longer than I know, or she has people in town. My gym is popular with the locals and the MC, but it's not known well beyond the borders of Valor.

"Saw it on my way through town." The tip of her tongue darts out to wet her pouty red lips. She smooths her hands down her dress, fidgeting with it like she's nervous again. A glimmer of anxiety shines in her eyes too. "Um...what position are you trying to fill?"

"You been in town long?" I ask, ignoring her question for the moment. Truth is, I wasn't hiring until two minutes ago. But if she needs work, I'll find a place for her. Having her close is all too appealing to me, for a thousand reasons I'm not ready to consider just yet.

"Only since last night. I'm staying at the...um..." Her eyes widen and she coughs like she's choking.

I fight back a smile. She's a terrible actress. Her cough is as fake as they come. She doesn't want me to know where she's staying, which is smart. Women can't ever be too careful. But there's only one suitable option in this town, the Meadowlark. I'm guessing that's where she spent the night.

"Shep Stratford," I say, holding out a hand to her.

She eyes it for a moment like she's worried it might bite her. And then she huffs a little breath and slips her hand into mine. As soon as her skin touches mine, electricity crackles against my skin. She feels it too and jumps as if I shocked her.

I bite the inside of my cheek to keep from cursing as my balls draw up tight and my dick throbs. Her hand is soft. Her nails are done in a light pink polish that shouldn't turn me on nearly as much as it does. I want to see those nails against my chest as she's riding me for broke.

Save a horse. Ride Shep.

Yeah, I like the sound of that.

"I'm Ainsley," she whispers. "Ainsley Foster. Are you sure you want to hire me?"

She seems worried, but I don't know why.

"How old are you, Ainsley?"

"Nineteen."

Thank you, Jesus.

"You ever answered phones before, lamb?"

"Yes, for my...last employer," she says.

I'd bet my left nut she was going to say something different and then thought better of it. She's a beautiful little liar, but a liar, nonetheless. And she's terrible at it.

Which is reassuring. It means she hasn't had a whole hell of a lot of practice at it. So I doubt she's running from the law or trying to pull some con. I'm guessing she's running from a rich daddy. Even though she's pure as the driven snow, there's a little spark of fire in her eyes, of rebellion. It's buried deep, but I see it in her.

It makes my balls throb in anticipation.

"You going to be here for a while?" I ask, not pushing her about her past. I want this girl to trust me. Actually, I need her to trust me on levels I didn't know existed until approximately four minutes ago.

"Yes." Her tongue darts out to touch her bottom lip again. It's a nervous habit and a tell. She isn't sure if she's telling me the truth or not. "I mean, I think so. If I can find work."

"Then the job is yours. Come by the gym this afternoon. I'll get you set up."

Rooster chuckles quietly and then wanders off. I already know I'll be getting shit for this for the foreseeable future. I don't even care though. Ainsley Foster is mine. She just doesn't know it yet.

"I can start today?" She seems excited by the prospect.

"Sure."

She squeaks like a little kitten and flings her arms around me. Her tits press against my chest, her sugar and vanilla scent hitting me like a Mack truck. I growl as cum shoots up my shaft and into my boxers. Fuck me. She's exactly as soft and sweet as I imagined.

"I'm so sorry!" she cries, jumping away from me. Her wide eyes meet mine, full of embarrassment. The same stains her cheeks. "I shouldn't have done that. Please don't fire me."

Fire her? Hell no. I'm keeping her.

By noon, I'm dying to see Ainsley again. I've spent the morning running all over the gym, trying to keep my mind off her. It didn't work. I'm anxious as hell she's going to change her mind and take off. She has that look about her...like she's already got one foot out the door, ready to make a run for it. I hope she doesn't try it. That'll just piss me off.

Don't think she'd be too thrilled with me if I spanked that round ass right out of the gate...which is exactly what will happen if I have to chase her down.

"Looking good," I call to Patriot, raising my voice so he hears me. He's one of our Prospects, the best one of the bunch as far as I'm concerned. He's partially deaf and always takes his hearing aid out while he's lifting. He says it gets wet and shuts off if he tries to leave it in.

He grins to let me know he heard me and then goes back to his set. He's working his ass off to push through his injuries from when two of this town's finest shot out his tires, causing him to wreck out a few weeks ago.

Patriot is turning into a hell of a man. He helps the club out with a lot of shit. He's been handling the phones around here when he's not busy with club business. In return, I train him for free and slip him a little cash. If Ainsley takes the job, I'll still pay him. There's always more work to do around here than bodies to do it. We stay busy.

This is the only gym in town, and I work hard to keep it clean. I don't love that the police department is right across the street, but this building was the only one big enough to fit my needs. And it allows me to help Savage, who owns the auto repair shop next to the cop shop, keep an eye on them.

This place used to be a movie theater. A couple of my Brothers helped me tear out the insides and renovate it. We did a hell of a job. The front wall is all glass. The floors are done up in club colors. Everything inside is brand new and state-of-the-art.

It's barely even one in the afternoon, but the place is packed. Rhonda is running her CrossFit class in the classroom. A couple of my Brothers are out back in the courtyard, working the ropes. Several women from town are lined up on the treadmills along the back wall...though half of them are busier watching Patriot than anything.

A lot of the women in town come here specifically to enjoy the show. But shit, their money spends like anyone else's, and my Brothers get a laugh out of it, so it's all good. I'll be putting a stop to that if it bothers Ainsley.

I know next to nothing about her, but she's already got me tangled up in knots. Something about her just feels...right. I'm not saying I believe in fate or destiny or any of that bullshit. But there's something about her that I haven't been able to shake all day.

If she doesn't show, I'm going to lose my mind.

She couldn't seem to get away fast enough after she hugged me this morning.

Rooster gave me nine kinds of hell about her. Like he can talk. He didn't waste any time locking down his ol' lady, Clover. Hell, half the club seems to be catching feelings lately. They all fell hard and fast. When you've seen the things we've seen and done the shit we've done, you learn quick what really matters in life. You learn to take your happiness where you get it, and you guard it close.

As far as I'm concerned, every one of my Brothers has earned the right to happiness. It's damn good to see the shit-eating grins they all walk around with these days.

I've given them all kinds of shit about it, but I can't even lie. I want what they've got. Bad. All my life, I've been alone. Thought I liked it that way until I joined up and found my first family. And then I fell in with the MC and found my second. Putting down roots here...it's been good for me in more ways than one.

I can see myself raising a family and growing old here. I've already decided I'll be doing that with Ainsley. Maybe that's fast. Maybe I'm crazy. Don't really give a shit. Those bright eyes of hers touched something inside of me that no one has ever touched before, lit up parts of me I didn't even know could light up like that.

I need to move slow with her. Give her time to get used to me. She's such a skittish little thing, nervous as hell. I don't want to spook her and send her running. Like I said, that'll just piss me off.

It's obvious she doesn't know much about the world. It's equally as obvious that she's smart. The combination of innocence and intelligence does things to do me I did not expect.

A...tingle goes up my spine.

I glance up just in time to see her walking in the door like a sign from above.

My dick reacts to her the exact same way he did this morning, raging to life like her own personal plaything. She changed out of her dress into a pair of pink yoga pants and a t-shirt. Her sneakers are pink and purple. She's so girly and cute. Never knew that could be so hot, but I like it a hell of a lot on her.

I should probably be ashamed of the fact that I've jerked off to thoughts of her twice already. I'm not. Sue me.

Ordinarily, I'd know everything there is to know about her by now. But I didn't look into her like I would anyone else. I want her to tell me what she's running from and why. I want her to trust me with her secrets.

I stride toward her, smiling as she gapes like she's never set foot inside a gym before. Her eyes bounce from one thing to another, trying to take it all in. I can tell when she comes across something she isn't familiar with. Her brows furrow and she tilts her head back and forth like she's trying to figure out what it is or how it works.

"You made it," I say, stopping right in front of her.

Her eyes lock with mine, her cheeks instantly turning pink. Those blue eyes seem to see right through me, warming places inside I didn't know could be warmed.

"Hi," she whispers, shyly. "I wasn't sure what time I should be here. You didn't say. I hope I'm not late. Or early." She grimaces. "I guess I'd rather be early than late though, right?"

"You're not early or late," I murmur, smiling as she rambles. "You're right on time."

"Oh, good." She exhales a relieved breath, her gaze darting around again. "This place is...wow. I've never been inside a gym like this before now. Oh. Maybe I shouldn't have said that."

"Hey," I murmur, reaching for her hand. Like this morning, as soon as my skin touches hers, a jolt goes through me. I like the way it feels. A whole helluva lot.

I tug her a step closer, until we're damn near sharing the same little sliver of air. She tips her head back, looking up at me with her pouty red lips parted. There's something in her eyes, a little spark that I want to set aflame just to see how hot she can get for me. It's the same one from earlier. There's a little minx in her. I can't wait to set it free.

"Easy, little lamb," I say, tilting my head closer to her. "I'm not going to fire you for not being familiar with a gym like this, all right?"

"Okay," she whispers.

"Come on, I'll show you around," I say, still holding onto her hand.

She notices and slips it from mine almost like she's been caught doing something wrong.

I scowl, instantly wanting her skin against mine again. Snatching her hand back would probably make her jumpy. I kind of want to do it though. I like touching her. Plus, there are other men here. If I'm holding her hand, they know she's off limits. It's a win-win.

"This is where you'll be working," I say, leading her to the front desk. It's spacious, with the Stratford logo emblazoned across the front of the counter so it's the first thing you see when you walk in the doors. "The phone system is simple, and we run everything through a booking program. It shouldn't take you too long to figure out how to operate it. It's pretty straightforward."

"I'm good with computers," she says, her voice soft but confident.

"Then you should pick this up with no problem. We do a little of everything here. Personal training, classes, and self-guided workouts." I place a hand on the small of her back, turning her to look out into the gym. I like the way my hand fits right above her ass and the way she shivers like she's enjoying it too. "To the right is the classroom. My office is on the left. The locker rooms and bathrooms are through the back. I've also got a courtyard out back for outdoor training."

"Wow," she whispers.

"See the man lifting weights?" I ask her, pointing toward Patriot.

She follows my gaze and nods.

"That's Patriot," I say. "He spends a lot of time around here, helps me out. If you ever need any-thing and can't find me, you go to Patriot."

"Patriot. Got it."

"My Brothers spend a lot of their time here. They have access codes to the building, so they come and go as they see fit. I'll make sure you know who they are," I mutter.

"You have brothers?"

"Sort of," I say, smiling at her question. "We're not blood-related. We're Men of Valor, an MC. Every-one is welcome here with the exception of law en-forcement."

She freezes beside me.

"The cops in this town are dirty," I explain quietly. "They have a bad habit of making themselves a nuisance to women. That shit doesn't fly here. I don't want them in here harassing anyone."

"Okay," she whispers and then turns her face up to me. Her eyes are wide, full of worry. "Um, you said MC. You mean MC like outlaw motorcycle club?"

"I mean motorcycle club. We're not what you see on the news."

She's so easy to read. The doubt in her eyes is plain as day.

"We aren't the Hells Angels," I murmur, tipping my head down toward her. My eyes lock with hers. "Most of us are ex-military. We help take care of shit around here."

"But you don't like cops."

"Not everyone who wears a uniform deserves one, Ainsley. Ask Patriot," I say, nodding at him. He's still grinding at the weight bench. "A few weeks ago, two of them shot out his tires and injured him. They tried to do some real fucked up shit to a teacher here in town."

That's just the tip of the iceberg, but I don't tell her that. I don't want to scare her into running. I just want her to be cautious about who she trusts. People see uniforms and feel safe. Here, that hasn't been a good thing for a long time.

"Did they get in trouble?"

"They were handled," I say carefully. She's already hesitant about MCs. I don't think she knows much about men like us, those willing to kill to protect what's ours. It's not something we relish doing. But sometimes, street justice is the only justice to be had. Especially when dirty cops are involved. I already know I would raze the police station to the fucking ground if they tried to hurt her. Avoiding that scenario is a good thing.

Her face pales slightly as she catches what I don't say and puts the pieces together.

Shit. I'm fucking this all up. The thought of her being afraid of me or my Brothers doesn't sit well with me. In fact, I don't like it at all. I want this girl to run into my arms, not flee in terror. She's sheltered, naïve...innocent in every sense of the word. I need to dial it back.

"You're safe with me, baby girl," I murmur, reaching out to run a hand down her arm. She startles slightly, but she doesn't pull away or run. "I will never let anything bad happen to you, do you understand?"

"I..." She trails off and nods, her blue eyes locked on mine like she can't look away. She knows I mean it though. I think she knows how *much* I mean it too. She doesn't look opposed to having me all up in her personal space. Which is a damn good thing. I need this girl to fall for me.

"I have a question, and I need you to be honest with me."

"Okay," she whispers.

"Are you in trouble?" The question erupts bluntly...but that's always been my way. Working intelligence, you learn that the things you say and the way you say them matter a whole hell of a lot. Assumption, insinuation, and implication can get someone killed in a hurry. So I don't pussyfoot around a topic. I say exactly what I mean, no more and no less. I'd rather her get used to that habit now than for it to cause problems later.

"What?"

"Are you in trouble, lamb? I know you're running from something. Hey." I quickly grab her arm when she starts to take a step away, shutting down on me. "Easy. I'm not asking you to tell me your story. I just want to make sure you're safe. If someone is trying to hurt you, I'll keep someone stationed here so you're protected while you're working. I can pay you under the table, keep your name off the record."

"No, I'm not in trouble," she whispers, her tone full of reluctance. "But maybe we can do the under-the-table thing?"

Her response leaves me with more questions than answers, but it's something, at least. Enough to ease my mind a bit and confirm what I worked out this morning.

"Yeah, lamb. We can do that. Let's go get you started," I say, dropping the subject.

The relief in her gaze is almost as clear as her relieved sigh. She's locked up tight, afraid to share whatever sent her running. But sooner or later, she'll realize she can trust me with her secrets.

She'll know that I would never betray or hurt her. And then I can make her mine.

Just, please, God, let it be soon because I'm already obsessed with this girl.

Chapter Two

"Whoa," I whisper, gaping at the bar in front of me. Midnight Oil is...something. It looks like a giant barn, but instead of being set in the middle of a field, a large parking lot surrounds the building. Motorcycles are lined up out front, with cars packed into the lot.

Strains of country music trickle out of the bar.

"You'll love it," Riley Pearce promises. She's my first friend in Valor and I really like her. She's a little older than I am, but she's really sweet. Like me, she's curvy, with dark hair and a past she doesn't talk about much. She convinced me to come out tonight instead of hiding in my motel room like I usually do after work.

"I've never been to a bar before," I murmur to her.

"Really? Never?"

"Nope. Never."

"I'm not a big fan of bars either," she admits. "But Midnight Oil isn't bad."

The bar seems popular enough. Finding parking is not easy. I circle the lot twice, looking for a spot.

I've been in Valor, Wyoming for two weeks. I'm not sure what made me stop here. Maybe it was the fact that the town is small and kind of...homey. It's the exact opposite of my life in Cheyenne. My uncle, Justice Foster, is the most powerful man in the state. He owns cattle ranches and business ventures all over the place, but I'm pretty sure he and my dad weren't always legitimate businessmen. I've heard whispers about the things they used to do.

That all changed when I was seven. My parents were shot by a man he and my dad put out of business. Neither of them survived.

Justice went legitimate, took custody of me...and immediately went overboard.

I've spent the last twelve years of my life tucked away on his estate, carefully guarded by his security team. I've wanted for nothing except freedom. If I left the property, I had guards. Even at the private school I attended, I had guards. Finding friends with a security detail watching over me wasn't easy. No one wanted to be followed around by three men with guns all the time.

People are still afraid of my uncle. They still whisper that he's dangerous.

Milan Cooper is the only real friend I've had until now. I met her when she switched schools our junior year. She's the only one Justice and my security team never scared away. I don't think she's afraid of much. Thank God.

I know Uncle Justice means well, and I love him to death. But the man who killed my parents died a long time ago. The same thing isn't going to happen to me. It's time Justice realizes that too.

So three weeks ago, Milan helped me escape. I spent the first week driving around aimlessly, not sure where I was going or what I was doing. I only had the cash we were able to scrape together and the clothes I was able to hide away at her house. I called home from the road once to let Justice know I'm okay. He was not happy when I wouldn't tell him where I was.

I've driven all the way to the state line twice, but I couldn't make myself cross it either time. I don't mean to worry him, but I wasn't built for the life he envisions for me. I don't want to spend my whole life in a glass bubble, able to look out but never able to touch the world as it passes by.

So that's what I'm doing. Experiencing life.

I like Valor. Everyone has been really nice and welcoming. They don't treat me with kid gloves like everyone did back home. I'm slow to warm up to most people, but I'm not delicate. I'm not going to break if someone raises their voice at me or says something I don't like. Everyone who worked for Justice acted like I would. No one ever told me how they really felt about anything. They just said what they thought I wanted to hear.

I hated it.

I may not know much about the world, but I'm not a little kid and I'm not stupid. Being treated like I'm still the traumatized seven-year-old I was when my parents died is frustrating. I feel like I'm closer to finding out what I'm capable of here than I ever was back in Cheyenne.

The part of Valor where Midnight Oil is located is old and run down. I always feel safer on this side of town than anywhere else, though. I think that's because of Shep Stratford. The Men of Valor are stationed on this side of town, and he makes sure they keep an eye on me without crowding me. They are...not at all what I expected.

When Shep told me he was in an MC, it made me nervous. The only thing I know about motorcycle clubs is what I've seen on TV or read in books. I expected his MC to be dangerous. I guess they can be when they need to be, but for the most part, they're regular people. Okay, that's not exactly true. They're insanely hot, ex-military regular people. Which probably doesn't rate as *regular* on any scale, but my point is...they're not bad guys.

And Valor already feels more like home to me than the mansion where I grew up. I know that's because of Shep. He's been so good to me. I wasn't sure what I expected when I walked into Rooster's diner my first morning in town, but Mrs. Witherbee, the nice lady who runs the motor court where I'm staying, said he might be hiring. When he said he wasn't, I wanted to cry. The money I have left won't go very far. Sleeping in my car sounds terrifying.

And then Shep swooped in to save the day.

I've never worked a day in my life aside from answering phones for Justice when his secretary quit. But I refuse to use any of my credit cards. I don't want Justice to be able to track me down. He'll make me go back home to my perfect little bubble and my half-life...and I'll die of boredom.

I want to stay here.

Because of Shep, a little voice in my mind whispers.

It's not entirely wrong. Shep is the strongest man I've ever met. Literally. Watching him work out at the gym he owns is always the highlight of my day. The way his body moves is fascinating to me! He is so damn sexy. He's tall and broad, with cinnamon brown eyes and crewcut brown hair. There's something wicked in his eyes that sends my entire body up in flames when he looks at me. He is dangerously hot.

His facial features look as if they were carved from granite. They're so sharp and severe. His entire *body* looks like it was carved from muscle. But he's not a gym rat like the ones Milan always complained about. He's crazy smart and has been nothing but sweet to me since day one.

I'm short and curvy, a size twenty. But I feel small next to him, and not in a bad way. He makes me feel like I'm protected without suffocating me. I feel like I'm allowed to be myself and say how I feel around him, and he won't judge me for it. He's very blunt, which I love.

Who am I kidding? I think I fell in love with him on day one.

I'm so afraid he's going to see it written all over my face! He's always watching me. Even when he's in his office, I feel his eyes on me. It makes me feel...wanted. Sexy. Safe. No one has ever given me butterflies before him.

I don't think he feels the same way about me though. Why would he?

The Men of Valor seem to like curvy women. A lot of them are paired up with women who look like me. But they don't own gyms like Shep does. He's a literal freaking giant, with muscles other men dream about.

He never makes me feel out of place or pressures me about my size though. I think the only reason he taught me how to use any of the equipment at all is because I asked him fifty million questions about it. He makes using it all look easy. I still struggle not to go flying off the treadmill when I accidentally turn the speed up too high. Having short legs is a lot of work.

He had to rescue me the only time I tried to use one of the new treadmills. I did not know they came with freaking Power Ranger mode! It did not end well for me. I panicked and forgot I could just pull the emergency cord to get it stopped.

Shep didn't laugh at me for it. He brought me pie and reprogrammed it so it would only go at my pace. I expected a guy who looks like him to be...well, a guy who looks like him. He's blunt, but he's always nice to everyone. He checks on me all the time, makes sure I don't need anything. Every morning, he brings me coffee from Rooster's. I don't think he has a mean bone in his body, even if he does have a wicked glower to rival Uncle Justice's.

I know he has questions about me, but he never asks them...which is a huge relief.

I'm not ready to tell him the truth. I don't think he'd be the way he is with me if he knew about my uncle. *Everyone* acts differently towards me once they know about Justice.

I hate it!

It's like they think he'll destroy them if they make one wrong move. And maybe he would. I don't know. He changed a lot after my parents died. The guilt almost destroyed him. But he still doesn't take crap from anyone. He doesn't expect everyone to fall at his feet, but people don't cross him. I don't know if he still does any of the things he did back then. To me, he's just...Uncle Justice. Rich as a king. Bossy as one too.

But he's not here now. I get to make my own rules and live life on my own terms for once. And I fully intend to enjoy every minute of my newfound freedom.

"Do you know how to line dance?" Riley asks.

I shake my head.

"It's okay. I didn't either my first time." She smiles at me. "It's easy to pick up. You just follow along with everyone."

"It sounds like fun," I promise her. "I'm more excited than nervous. I've never been out like this before. It's exciting."

She raises a brow, surprised. But she doesn't ask for an explanation. It's one of the things I love about her. She never pries for information. I met her at the grocery store in town last week. I think she knew I was struggling to figure out what to buy. Nema, our cook, always did the grocery shopping and cooking at home. I didn't even know there were so many brands of canned vegetables...which is all the proof I need to know running was the right thing to do.

What nineteen-year-old doesn't know how to grocery shop?

Me. That's who.

But Riley took pity on me and helped me figure out what I needed, and what I could even cook in my motel room. Turns out...not a whole lot. I managed to find a few things I could heat in the microwave or on the hot plate. And Riley offered to help me find more long-term housing if I need it.

I'm beginning to think that's a good idea. I plan to take her up on her offer as soon as I can afford something more permanent.

I love Mr. and Mrs. Witherbee, but my motel room does not offer a lot of space. I feel a little claustrophobic if I spend too much time in it. Which is exactly why I agreed to go out with Riley tonight. It's Friday. Going out is what girls my age do on Fridays. Or so I've been told. Milan and I never really went out. She didn't date, and it wasn't even an option for me. Uncle Justice would have scared off any potential date before they even crossed the threshold.

No one ever tried anyway. I'm nineteen and I've never been kissed. I've never held hands with a man or flirted with one. All I know about dating and men, I learned from television and from living with Justice. And he never brought women home. Sometimes, when I was quiet and sneaky enough, I could eavesdrop on my security team talking about the women in their lives.

I didn't listen much. They were very...boastful.

It made looking them in the eyes super awkward.

"Come on then," Riley says, smiling at me. "Let's go line dancing!"

I giggle at her exuberant tone and pull in beside a beat-up Honda. Gravel crunches beneath the tires of my car...Milan's car. She gave me hers when I left so Justice couldn't track me through it. I'm sure mine is probably GPS chipped. But even her car stands out here. It's a brand-new Mercedes SL. I keep the roof up in town and haven't washed the road muck off so it blends in a little better, but it still sticks out like a sore thumb.

Riley and I make our way toward the front of the bar. My eyes drift toward the motorcycles lined up. They all look so sleek and fast. Justice owns one, but I don't think I've ever seen him actually ride it. Shep always rides his. His bike is gorgeous. It's red and black with little flashes of chrome that draw the eye. He looks like a warrior riding it.

Disappointment whispers through me when I don't see his bike with the others. I really like Riley, but I kind of agreed to come hoping he would be here tonight even though I'm pretty sure this isn't his scene. He doesn't like to be around a lot of people. Whenever he goes to Rooster's, he always sits in the same booth in the very back, his back against the wall. He's more relaxed at the gym, but even then, he always seems to know exactly where everyone is inside the building, and rarely ever leaves his back to the door.

I've noticed a lot of guys in the MC are the same way. I'm guessing it's some leftover defense mechanism from their days in the military. They guard their backs, make sure no one is able to sneak up on them. I can't even imagine the sorts of things they've seen over the years.

"He won't be here," Riley murmurs from beside me, her voice quiet. "Shep doesn't drink so he never comes here unless the Brothers drag him here."

"Oh." I pause. "Is it that obvious?"

"That you're in love with him?" She waits for me to nod. "Only a little. He's a good guy."

"Yeah, he is."

"Are you going to tell him how you feel?" she asks.

"God no." I rapidly shake my head.

She smiles at me like she understands. She doesn't press for more or laugh at the thought of Shep with someone who looks like me.

"Come on. Let's go dance the night away," she says, jogging up the steps.

I hang back for a second, scanning the parking lot just to make sure Riley isn't wrong about him never coming here. I can't help it! I enjoy being around him...and maybe I want to dance with him.

Honestly though, he looks more like the kind of man who would drag me into the bathroom to have his dirty way with me versus one who would dance. Sometimes, I think I see desire in his dark eyes when he looks at me. That's probably just wishful thinking. I don't even know what the heck desire is supposed to look like. He looks...hungry sometimes though. Like he's thinking about dragging me into his office to eat me for lunch.

I'm not so sure I would mind if he did. Until him, I never really cared about the fact that I've never dated. Now I wish I were brave enough to ask him out. I'm not, of course. Are you kidding? I'd probably die of mortification.

Here lies Ainsley Foster, the clueless virgin who choked on her own tongue.

A wall of noise hits me when Riley pulls the door open. The bar is loud and crowded, but not overwhelmingly so. Country music blares through the speakers. People are dancing on one side of the room. Tables are set up along the other. Loud bursts of laughter sound over the music, which makes me smile. Everyone seems to be having a good time.

And I'm going to have one too.

Even if I do secretly wish I were at the gym, watching Shep workout.

"Hey, Patriot," I say, smiling when he walks up to the booth where I'm sitting. I lost track of Riley a while ago. I think she might have left. She reacted a little oddly when she saw the hot stranger talking to Bullet, the President of the MC. The hot stranger turned out to be Clint Bolton, or Bolt. He's incredibly good-looking but not at all my type...which is basically Shep and only Shep.

When we went over to say hello, there was a weird tension between Riley and Bolt. He couldn't take his eyes off her, and even though she was trying to hide it, she couldn't seem to take hers off him either. She disappeared not long later.

I don't mind. She was clearly rattled by Bolt. I don't know why, but there's a story there. I'll call later to make sure she made it home safely. I won't push her if she doesn't want to talk, but if she does, I can listen. I owe her that much.

Since she left, I've just been sitting, enjoying the music. Okay, that's not true. I've been dragging my feet about leaving, hoping Shep shows up. Several more of his Brothers have trickled in over the last hour or so, but he wasn't with them.

"Hey, Ainsley," Patriot shouts over the music, leaning down so he can hear me. He's my age and is really sweet. I like him. He keeps a polite distance though. All the Brothers do. I'm not really sure why, and I'm not nearly brave enough to ask. I don't really mind it anyway.

"You been having fun?" Patriot asks.

"Yeah," I shout over the music. "I think I'm going to leave soon. I'm kind of tired."

"You need a ride, babe?" the guy with him asks. I've never met him before. He's young, maybe twenty-five or twenty-six. His dark hair is a little greasy and his beard looks unkempt. His gaze roves over me, his green eyes darkening. I don't think he means me any harm, but I don't like the way he's looking at me.

I tug my skirt down, trying to make it longer to hide my thighs from him.

"No thanks," I say.

"Slate, this is Ainsley. Ainsley, Slate," Patriot shouts, introducing us.

"Hi," I murmur, tilting my face up and giving Slate a polite smile.

He takes it as encouragement.

He leans down, putting his face close to mine. His eyes are dilated, and I can smell the alcohol on his breath as he grins at me. "Do you want something to drink before you go, babe?"

God, no. I've had champagne and wine before, but I don't care for alcohol. Besides, I'm not even old enough to drink. There's no way I'm going to risk anyone getting in trouble for serving me. Avoiding the police seems like a good idea. Not just because Shep doesn't trust them, but because I don't want them calling my uncle.

I scoot away, but he follows me, getting so close he's practically in the booth with me. My heart pounds, fear shooting through me.

I think Patriot notices.

"Slate, man, back up," he warns Slate.

"We're cool. Aren't we, babe?" Slate asks me, his words slurred. His breath touches the side of my face again, and then his hand does. He leans so close I think he's going to try to kiss me.

Anxiety bubbles up hard and fast. My stomach churns.

Before I can tell him to back up, he's gone. One minute he's right there, too close for comfort. The next, he's not. I glance up, trying to figure out what just happened. My heart leaps when I catch sight of Shep, his hand clutched in the back of Slate's black t-shirt, holding Slate away from me.

The look on his face is pure murder.

"Shep, man," Slate says, holding up his hands. "I was just talking to her."

"Don't," Shep says, that single word cutting through the noise like the crack of a whip. "Don't talk to her. Don't look at her. And if you ever think about touching her again, we're going to have problems. You feel me?"

"Yeah, I got it."

Shep gives him a hard glare and then releases him.

Slate stumbles before he catches himself.

"C'mon, Slate. It's time to go," Patriot says, nudging Slate to get him moving. He shoots Shep an apologetic look and then gives me the same.

I'm not mad at him. He didn't know his drunk friend was going to touch me.

He leads Slate away from me. I make a mental note to keep a whole lot of distance between us if I ever see him again. I don't think he meant to hurt me, but he scared the crap out of me. No one has ever gotten that close to me before...except Shep. And Shep didn't make me want to crawl under the table to escape. When he touches me, my entire body sings the *Hallelujah Chorus*.

Shep stands right where he's at, his feet planted apart and his chest heaving as he takes deep breaths. His hair is damp. He looks gorgeous in his tight t-shirt with his cut over it and faded jeans.

My gaze crawls all over him like I haven't seen him in days instead of mere hours.

He stares at me like he's mad at me, his jaw clenched tight enough to crack.

Unease trickles through me. Am I in trouble for coming here? I hope not. I know I'm underage, but Patriot is here. He's the same age as me. And I didn't drink anything.

"Thank you," I whisper, figuring one of us should probably say something.

"Let's go," he barks, holding out a hand to me.

Crap. He is really mad.

Even though he's angry, I'm not afraid of him. Slipping my hand in his and letting him pull me to my feet feels completely natural. The heat coming off his body scorches me.

My legs tremble beneath me like I'm a newborn colt just learning to stand. I remember the way his body felt pressed to mine the first day I met him, and my entire body breaks into a sweat. He's hard everywhere. And he smells freaking amazing, like soap and leather and sunshine.

I fight back the moan threatening to break free, desperately trying not to embarrass myself.

"Motherfucker," he swears, his gaze dropping to my dress.

"What?" I glance down, but I can't see anything out of place. My black bodycon dress has a retro look to it, with roses painted on each side at the waist. It's form-fitting, but it's not short or anything. It ends at midthigh. It's tighter than what I usually wear, but I like the way it flatters my curves. Milan gave it to me.

"I'm burning that dress so you can't wear it again," Shep growls, clearly not liking the way I look in it.

My stomach sinks, a little piece of my heart cracking. I turn for the door, my head down to hide the humiliation burning in my cheeks and threatening to leak from my eyes.

I guess I'm not his type. He didn't have to be so mean about it though.

Chapter Three

Ainsley is dead silent beside me as I lead her through the bar. I've spent the last two weeks trying to keep my hands off her. It has me wound so tightly I'm ready to snap. Seeing Slate with his hand on her didn't help. Neither did the genuine fear in her eyes when he touched her. I wanted to drive my fist into his face and then wrap my hand around his throat. He's lucky she was watching, or I may have done just that.

When Nova called after Church to tell me that Ainsley was here, I was not thrilled. She's not old enough to drink. And even though the bar is club owned, it can still get rough at times. It's no place for a girl like her.

Nova didn't fucking warn me that she looks like pure sex. Her form-fitting dress has my dick so hard walking is painful. Her body has starred in every fantasy I've had for the last two weeks. She is the sexiest little thing I've ever met, and she is completely oblivious to it.

Pres. catches my eye and arches a brow, silently asking if everything is cool.

I jerk my chin in a nod, leaving it at that.

Slate isn't a bad guy. Like Patriot, he's one of our Prospects. Ordinarily, I like the guy. But he needs to learn to keep his fucking hands to himself before he loses them. I don't know if he's always so aggressive with women when he drinks, but I intend to find out. That shit won't be happening again, especially not to Ainsley.

But I'll talk to Bullet about that later. I've spent every waking moment of the last two weeks watching Ainsley, obsessing over her. She's soft-hearted. Club business or not, if she thought Slate was in trouble for flirting with her, she'd be upset about it. And I can tell by the way she keeps her head down that she's already upset. I'm just not sure why.

She looked relieved when she saw me. Her expression didn't change until I threatened to burn her dress. Maybe it's got some sentimental value or something? I don't know. If she wants to keep it, I'm not going to stop her. But she won't be wearing it again where anyone else can see her.

It's too sexy, and she's already sexy enough. God, is she ever. She is so damn pretty. I spend half my time just staring at her because I can't look away. Every expression that crosses her face is fascinating to me. She's so easy to read, so genuine. You can tell just by looking at her what she thinks about any given subject.

When she's happy, she glows. When she's worried or nervous, her tongue peeps out. She fidgets when she's uncomfortable and cleans when she's bored or feeling antsy. Every time she figures out how to work something on her own, she laughs, lighting up the entire gym.

When Rhonda is running CrossFit, she enjoys watching. She likes to watch when I'm at the weight bench too. I've always worked out, but I've been a machine the last two weeks, trying to work off the sexual frustration.

It's not working. As soon as I feel her eyes on me, I want to lay her out over the bench and work out a few different muscles...like my tongue and my cock. Preferably in that order. The things I want to do to this girl would probably send her running for the hills if she knew. I'm a dirty son of a bitch for even thinking them. But I've had two weeks to resign myself to that fact. It is what it is. There isn't a spot on her body I won't have my mouth all over as soon as I can make it happen.

I've never wanted anyone as badly as I want her. I've never felt possessive or jealous or like I need to stamp my name all over her body so everyone knows she's taken. With her, the feeling never subsides. I gave her a stack of t-shirts that say *Stratford Training and Fitness*, just so I'd have my name on her. I still want my patch on her. I still want my marks on her. I still want my ring on her and my kid in her belly. When clients at the gym smile at her, I think of about eight different places to hide their bodies so they're never found. I am completely gone over this girl...and she doesn't have a clue. It's enough to drive me insane.

"My car is over here," she says when we step out onto the porch of the bar, moving like she's going to go left.

"And my bike is over here," I say, steering her to the right. When Nova called, I briefly considered bringing my cage so Ainsley would be comfortable. But the thought of having her body pressed to mine was too tempting. If that makes me a bastard, so be it.

I've been trying to go slow and give her time since I met her. I'm not trying anymore. Now I'm going to enjoy making her sweat. This little lamb is mine. It's about time she knows it too. Please, *God*, let her figure it out soon. Preferably before I have to kill some motherfucker for touching what doesn't belong to him.

"I can't ride your motorcycle," she says, gaping at me. "I'm in a dress."

"You've been in a bar. You can't drive," I say, even though I know she's sober. Nova said she drank water all night. But telling her she can't drive isn't a lie...exactly. She can't drive because I want her on the back of my bike. If I end up in hell, a little white lie isn't going to be what sends me there, so I'm not even sweating it.

"I wasn't drinking, Shep," she says, her blue eyes wide and earnest. "I know you're mad at me for coming here, but I promise I wouldn't do anything to put you or the club at risk. I just wanted to get out of my motel room for a little while."

"Good to know," I mutter, tugging on her hand to get her moving. "But you were in the bar, you're underage, and the cops love to sit down the street and fuck with people. I'd rather not give them a reason to think they should raid the place."

Her face pales as if she never even considered that. She looks stricken, guilty.

That wasn't what I was going for. I'm not mad at her. I'm fucking livid that Slate put his hands on her, that he scared her...that he saw her in a dress I want to see on my bedroom floor. I open my mouth to tell her she didn't do anything wrong, but she blinks and looks away from me, headed toward my bike.

She glances around the whole time, trying to be furtive about it and failing miserably. I think she expects the cops to jump out of the shadows at any minute. It's cute as hell. The way she leans into me eases a little of the possessive jealousy roiling through me.

Slate may have touched her face, but it'll be me she's pressed up against for the next ten minutes. It'll be me making those nipples hard and her clit ache. It'll be me dropping her off at her door tonight. There is no bad here.

"You ever been on a bike before, Ainsley?" I ask, grabbing the helmet I brought for her.

She eyes it like it's liable to bite her. Which is cute as all hell too. Ainsley doesn't share much about herself. If any given conversation gets too close to anything personal, she shuts down lickety-split. But I've learned enough over the last two weeks to know she's exactly as sheltered as I suspected that first day. She eats up every new experience like she's starving for it.

I'm guessing her daddy kept her under lock and key. She's too pure for this world, too sweet. And if I'm a bastard for wanting to be the one who corrupts her, then I'll wear that title. Because I plan to do a whole lot of corrupting. Starting with getting her on the back of my bike.

"No," she says, chewing on her bottom lip. "Which is pretty strong evidence that we should take my car. I'm not very coordinated, Shep. What if I fall off or make you wreck or something? Better not to risk it."

"We're taking my bike, lamb."

"Fine," she huffs, snatching the dome out of my hands. "But if we die, it's your fault."

"We're not going to die," I say with a soft chuckle.

That seems to piss her off more. She yanks the helmet on over her head, scowling like she wants to set me on fire. Her attitude only makes my dick harder. One day soon, I'm going to piss her off just so I can tumble her to the floor and fuck her raw.

"I'll get on first, and then I want you to slide on behind me. Use the pegs. Sit close to me and wrap your arms around my waist," I instruct her. "You'll be perfectly safe."

"I can't straddle the bike," she gasps as if just remembering why she objected to me taking her home in the first place. "Everyone will see my butt."

That right there almost has me agreeing to take her cage. Almost. But the parking lot is clear. Everyone is still inside enjoying themselves.

"Here," I say, delving my hand into one of the pannies on my bike and pulling out my jacket for her to use to cover herself. It's chilly out, so she needs it anyway.

"That's not going to fit me," she mumbles, her cheeks turning pink. She dips her head so the top of the dome hides her eyes from me.

"Try it, baby girl," I murmur, uneasy at the look on her face. She seems almost...embarrassed.

Does her body bother her? It certainly doesn't bother me. If anything, I like it a little too much. I spend a good sixteen hours a day thinking about it. The other eight, I dream about it. Besides, I'm a hell of a lot bigger than she is. The jacket will fit her.

"It'll keep anyone from seeing your panties."

She takes the jacket from me and quickly shoves her arms into it. As expected, it swallows her. I wait for her to look at me again, but she studiously avoids my gaze. I give up for the moment and straddle the only other woman in my life, my custom Ducati.

Ainsley slides on behind me, moving like she expects the bike to bite her. Or maybe it's me she thinks is feral. She certainly tries to sit as far back as she can without falling off the ass-end. I fight a smile at that and reach back to grab her legs.

She jolts upward, nearly unseating both of us.

"Easy, lamb," I croon. "I'm just going to slide you forward. Get as close to me as you can."

Please, get as close to me as you can. Let me feel the heat coming off that virgin cunt.

She huffs again and then inches forward little by little.

I almost cum in my jeans when she slides her arms around me, her palms splayed across my abdomen. Jesus, that feels good. And I'm definitely going to hell for trying to will her into sliding them lower to touch my cock.

She doesn't, which is a damn shame. All it'd take at this point is one innocent graze to get me off. I've never been this hard up for pussy. I went without for years with no problem and no regrets. But one look at her, and I'm willing to beg if it gets her into my bed sooner.

And it's not just that I want to ride her hard. I want to plant my kid in her belly so badly it's almost pathetic. The thought of being the one to make this girl a mommy has had me ready to blow for days. One of the teachers in town brought her little girl to the gym on Monday. The girl spent the entire time following Ainsley around the gym. Ainsley was incredible with her.

I could tell by the look on her face that she wants kids. Desperately.

She'll make a hell of a mom when I give them to her.

Her thighs cinch around my hips. Just that fast, my raw emotions settle. My balls damn near give up the fight. I instantly decide she'll be on my bike with me at every available opportunity for at least the next seventy years, minimum. Her body is soft and warm, her sugar and vanilla scent just strong enough to make my mouth water.

She jolts again when I start the bike. Her thighs cinch even tighter, her hands fisting into my shirt like she's afraid the bike is going to try to peel her off me. My smile grows big enough to split my cheeks. I can't fucking wait to experience the world through this girl's eyes.

"Hold on," I murmur, already knowing this is going to be my easiest ride yet. Hell, everything about being around her is easy. Peaceful. Perfect.

She screams when I take off, clinging to me as hard as she can. By the time we hit the road though, her screams have given way to laughter. The sweet sound hits me in the heart, tumbling it right into her perfect little hands.

I take the long way through town, enjoying the way she's pressed up against me and the sound of her delighted laughter. It's so pure and sweet. I've never been sure before if God is real. But there's no way in hell Ainsley Foster was a simple coincidence. She's too damn perfect to have been anything other than hand crafted, stitched together with the best ingredients the universe had to offer.

Riding has always been my favorite thing to do. There's nothing like the feel of my bike between my thighs and the wind on my face. I find clarity when I'm riding. It soothes even the rawest places inside of me, those old wounds left from a childhood as a castaway kid and the more recent ones that mark anyone who has been to war.

With Ainsley on the back of my bike, I find heaven. It's a level of contentment I never knew existed before this moment, one that goes soul deep. I can't wait for her to fall in love with me. We'll go anywhere she wants to go, do anything she wants to do, just so I can keep her tucked up against me like this.

I slow outside the driveway for the Meadowlark and then pull in. Most of the lights are out but the place is impossible to miss. It's pink with bright blue doors, the bold colors striking and a little eccentric. But the Witherbees are good people. They keep the place clean and take care of their guests. I know Ainsley is in good hands here.

I wish like hell I were taking her back to my place instead.

I think I want to cuddle with this girl in my bed as badly as I want to bend her over the side of it and eat her little holes from behind. Simple intimacies like washing her hair or making her breakfast sound like a dream come true. My Brothers would probably laugh their asses off if they knew how badly I wanted to run a brush through her hair and then tuck her into bed with me.

Hell, maybe they'd get it.

I pull up in front of the door to her room and kill the engine.

Ainsley untangles her body from mine, moving slow enough to make me wonder if she didn't enjoy being pressed up against me as much as she enjoyed the ride itself. Once I'm sure she's steady, I slide off the bike and then help pull her to her feet.

She stumbles into me. My arms wind around her, pulling her close.

Her sweet little sigh and the way her body melts into mine lets me know I've got it right. She's into me. I just need to get her on the same page I'm on. Quickly.

"That was amazing, Shep," she says, tilting her head back so she can see me.

I help pull the dome off her head. Static electricity has strands of her hair floating upward as if they intend to stay inside the helmet. And then the wind catches them, flinging them all around her face. Not even the poor light filtering down from the streetlights hides the flush to her cheeks.

"Yeah? You enjoyed it?"

She nods, snuggling deeper into my jacket. It looks a helluva lot better on her than it does on me. She's keeping it. I've got others. And if anyone gives me shit for her wearing an MC jacket, well...she's not the only woman in town sporting one these days.

Men may not always be smart, but we're not stupid either. Nothing shouts *taken* quite like your woman walking around in your shit. Until I get a patch of her own on her, this will do just fine. Make sure there are no more issues like tonight. Maybe keep those fuckers who come to the gym from smiling at her all the time too.

"I did." She brushes her hair out of her face so she can see me again. "Um, thank you for bringing me—" Her lips purse, her brows furrowing in confusion. "How did you know where I'm staying?"

"You told me," I lie.

"Oh." She thinks about that a minute and then shrugs like it's possible she told me. She didn't. But

Valor isn't a big town. By now, half the town knows who she is and where she's staying. I just happened to know sooner than most. What? I'm nosy.

"Well, thank you for bringing me home. I guess I'll see you tomorrow."

"You don't have to come in tomorrow. You're allowed to take a day off," I murmur, reaching out to brush another wayward strand of hair away from her face. I let my knuckles trail along her cheek, wanting it to be my hand she remembers there and not Slate's. Unlike with him, she doesn't go taut or look afraid. She sways a little closer, almost as if in a dream.

"I like spending time at the gym," she admits, her voice whisper quiet. The way she says it makes it sound like she likes something in particular about being there.

Me? I sure as hell hope so.

"Sleep in tomorrow, Ainsley. Come in when you feel like it, all right?" I twist to the side to set the helmet on the back of the bike. "You've been working your ass off. You don't have to prove anything to me or anyone else. The job is yours as long as you want it."

"Okay." She licks her lips, her gaze flitting across my face. "Um, goodnight, Shep." She tries to take a step away, but I snag her hand before she can. "Is—"

I cut her off, pressing my lips to hers in a hard kiss. Hers are soft beneath mine, her breath sweet.

It takes every ounce of willpower I possess not to thrust my hand into her hair and devour her alive. I want to do it, so badly it's almost torture. But I don't.

I flick my tongue against her lips, taking a small taste of her. And then I back off.

"Goodnight, lamb," I murmur.

She stands there for a long minute, dazed.

"Go on in, Ainsley. It's cold out here."

"Oh!" she says like she's worried about me. I'm not cold though. That one little taste of her has my blood heated to the flash point. She goes to shrug out of my jacket, but I quickly shake my head.

"Keep it. You'll need it on Sunday."

"On Sunday?" Her brows furrow.

"Yeah, Sunday."

"Oh." She eyes me for a minute and then her curiosity gets the better of her. "Um...what's happening on Sunday?"

"Our first date, baby girl."

Her eyes get big.

I chuckle at her expression, leaning down to brush my lips across her forehead. "Go inside before you get cold, Ainsley. I'll see you in the morning."

She stands there for a minute and then shakes her head. Her lips curve into the tiniest smile. "Goodnight, Shep," she whispers.

"Sweet dreams, baby girl."

Chapter Four

"Here," Shep says, startling me. I glance up to find him standing on the other side of the front desk, holding out a cup of coffee toward me. Lord, he's far too good-looking in a tight t-shirt with the gym logo stretched across his chest and Navy sweats. The smile on his face makes my heart thump against my ribcage like a mallet rebounding off a gong. He seems cool as a cucumber, as if our kiss last night was no big deal.

I'm not remotely close to cool or cucumbery over it. I barely slept all night. Every time I managed to get comfortable, I would think about his lips on mine or the feel of his body against mine and my body would burst into flames again. Touching myself didn't help. I couldn't seem to get myself there, as usual.

Honestly, I don't know why I even try. Milan swears that women should know how to pleasure themselves. I've done it before, but since I got here, whenever I try, I just end up more frustrated. I don't know why I can't make myself come anymore...but I have a feeling it has to do with the gorgeous man standing in front of me.

My body wants him and only him, apparently.

I finally gave up trying to sleep at six this morning. Even though Shep told me to come in late, I got here at the same time I normally do. I was driving myself crazy staring at the walls of my room.

"My car," I blurt, the first words that come to mind.

His smile grows. "What about it?"

"It was outside the motel this morning."

"Mmhmm," he hums, taking a sip from his coffee cup.

"How? I have my keys."

"I have a certain set of lucrative skills."

"You hotwired it?" I gape at him, shocked. Though I'm not sure why. Shep is...not like anyone I have ever met before. In more ways than one. There's not much he can't do, as far as I can tell. He's so capable, so calm.

Last night is the only time I've ever seen him angry about something. I thought it was me, but I'm starting to think he was pissed off at Slate. He didn't seem mad when he kissed me. He growled like a big cat. The heat banked in his eyes made my knees weak.

"Nah. I borrowed a transponder key from Savage at the shop." He takes another sip of coffee, eyeing me over the rim of his mug. "You're here early."

"I couldn't sleep," I mumble and then take a big swallow of coffee to hide my blazing cheeks.

Judging by the sexy smirk that crosses his face, it doesn't work. Somehow, he always seems to know exactly what I'm thinking. It's frustrating! Trying to read him is like trying to read a foreign language upside down. His sharp features give away nothing. His eyes are so warm though, exactly like cinnamon.

"Were you thinking about our kiss, baby girl?"

I open my mouth to say...I have no idea what. I nod instead.

"Me too," he mutters, his eyes locking on my lips. "I knew you were going to taste like heaven, Ainsley. I kiss you again, I might get myself addicted."

"Do..." I stop and take a breath, reaching deep for a little courage to ask my question. If I don't, it'll drive me crazy. "Do you want to kiss me again?"

The words emerge in a soft whisper, but he hears them.

"Been thinking about it since the second my mouth left yours last night," he growls.

So have I. Obsessively.

"Can I ask you a question?" I ask, shoving my hands underneath my bottom to keep from fidgeting. I lock my eyes on Shep's broad chest, not sure I want to see his expression while we have this conversation.

"Ask away, little lamb," he says, drumming his fingers on the desk.

"Why did you hire me?" I whisper. Of course my cheeks heat as soon as the question leaves my lips. My stomach clenches, my nerves jangling. "I mean...I don't exactly look like I belong at the front desk of a gym. I know I'm—"

"Fucking beautiful."

I jerk my head up at the sound of his growl. My gaze tangles with his, and I swallow hard. Lord, he looks mad. His eyes blaze with heat, anger stamped into every gorgeous line of his face.

"You're fucking beautiful, Ainsley," he says, his voice as heated as his eyes. "You think you don't belong because you've got curves? Baby girl, those curves of yours are sweet enough to make a man crazy. Believe me, I know. I'm the one who dragged you out of the bar last night because I couldn't fucking stand for anyone else to look at you the way I do."

"H...how do you look at me?"

"Like a man who can't see anything but you," he growls, leaning over the desk toward me. His eyes prowl all over my body. I feel them like a brand on my skin, searing me in places no one has ever touched before, in ways I've never felt before.

My whole life, I've been sheltered, spoiled, pampered...and so damn lonely. Longing bubbles up from those deep-down places that brought me here in the first place, the ones that made me run, emerging from my lips in a whimper.

"You belong here, Ainsley," Shep says, reaching out to touch the side of my face. "This gym, this town, this is your home now. You'll never belong anywhere more than you belong right here with me."

"Shep," I whisper, my voice shaking. All of me is shaking, aching to feel his skin against mine, not just on my cheek, but everywhere. I've been in love with him since I walked through the front door of this place. But I never thought...I never knew... God, maybe I'm blind.

"Sooner or later, you'll let me in," he says, his voice softer now.

"Shep, I..." I want to tell him so badly about my uncle, about why I'm here and what I'm running from, but the words die on my lips, the truth refusing to come. Everyone is afraid of my uncle. As soon as they hear his name, they crack, and I end up right back in a glass bubble. Protected. Pampered. *Miserable.* I don't want Shep to crack. I don't want to have to look at him from inside my perfect little cage.

I want to stay right here with him because he's right...this is where I belong.

"It's okay, lamb. I got time." He touches my bottom lip, and smiles in reassurance. "I'm not going anywhere, baby girl. Promise you that."

His words ease a little of the guilt rushing through me.

"I want to tell you," I say, glancing down at my cup. "But I'm afraid."

"Of me?"

"No. Yes." I huff out a breath and then shrug. "I don't know."

"I won't hurt you, Ainsley," he murmurs, touching my cheek again.

I glance up at him again, the promise in his eyes sapping every bit of moisture out of my mouth.

"You're safe with me," he says, stroking my cheek with his thumb. His hands are rough, calloused, but they feel so good against my skin. "You're safe with my Brothers. We will fight like hell to keep you safe."

"I know you guys are good guys. That's not what I'm afraid of," I say.

"Then what?"

I shrug helplessly.

"Talk to me, Ainsley," he murmurs. "What's going on behind those pretty eyes?"

"I don't know." My thoughts are all tangled up like a briar patch. When I try to grab one, I hit another thorn. If I tell him why I'm afraid, I have to tell him about Uncle Justice. And if I do that...well, then maybe my fears come true, and I lose him. I'm not ready to lose him yet.

He's something I've never had before. He's...home, I think. For the first time in my life, I fit somewhere. I *belong* somewhere. Justice gave me everything, but he couldn't make me fit. Not on his cattle ranches, not in his mansion, or at the fancy schools I attended. Ever since my parents died, I've been adrift, unanchored and unmoored.

Shep makes me feel like I have a place and a purpose and a future here. If I lose that...if I lose *him*...I'm pretty sure it's going to destroy me. I've never wanted much. I've never asked for anything. But I want him and the life I'm building here, so badly I'm terrified of losing it.

"I'm sorry," I whisper, tears burning at the backs of my eyes.

"Don't be," he murmurs, his deep voice soft, full of understanding and patience. "I'm not mad at you, lamb. I've got all the time in the world." He holds his hand out to me. "Come on. I've got something to show you."

I take his hand, allowing him to help me to my feet. He pulls me around the desk, leaving his coffee on top as we pass by, headed deeper into the gym. Usually by now, a few of his Brothers are here. Shep and the guys who help him with the personal training clients work them hard. They all tease and give each other hell the whole time. I love seeing the camaraderie between them. He calls them his Brothers, which is fitting. It really is like they're family.

This morning, the gym is quiet, empty. Shep leads me toward his office, still holding my hand. I don't try to pull it away. I love how our hands fit together, our fingers linked as if they were made to be that way. His hand is so much bigger than mine, so much rougher.

I can't help but think about having it on other parts of my body. He's so big and hard everywhere. He's also very much used to being the one calling the shots. As sweet as he is to me, I can't quite imagine him being soft and flowery if he were touching me. I kind of think he'd be demanding and a little rough. I'm not sure if that should excite me, but it does.

Sweet and gentle or rough and bossy, I want him exactly as he is. Because from where I'm standing? He's pretty damn perfect.

His office is fascinating to me. It's so neat and orderly. Even the equipment he keeps stacked in the far corner is neatly organized. His desk is massive, but I don't think he likes spending time at it. He never lasts more than half an hour or so before he's up, checking on things, moving around. He doesn't like to sit still.

I'm pretty sure half the women who come here do so just to watch him and his Brothers workout. It's not hard to see why. They're all hot. Shep just happens to be the hottest, at least to me. He's so beautiful to me.

The door leading to the stairs is standing open. He pulls me toward it, sending my curiosity spiking. I know he lives upstairs, but I've never been up there before. He usually keeps the door locked so people don't wander into his place. I'm excited to see his personal space.

The stairwell is wide and well-lit. The walls and floors are painted like the gym, in MC colors. The landing at the top is almost big enough to be considered a foyer instead of a landing. There's only one door.

"This is my place," he murmurs, releasing my hand to open the door.

His apartment is massive. The ceilings are high, making it seem even bigger. So does the open floorplan. The hardwood floors and exposed gray brick outer walls look beautiful together. His furniture is modern, simple, with thick rugs giving each individual area a little definition.

"It's beautiful, Shep," I murmur, instantly falling in love with it. Despite being a little spartan, the space is bright and warm, inviting. The only personal detail is a giant mural of a motorcycle over the couch. It works though. It's very...him.

"It's functional," he says. "I plan to build. Got some property outside of town but haven't gotten to it yet. I've been more focused on the gym the last couple years." His gaze flickers over me. "I'll be fixing that sooner rather than later."

"I always dreamed about building my own house," I say.

"Yeah? What would you build?"

"A farmhouse with a wraparound porch and lots of windows."

"You want a farm?" he asks, tugging me deeper into his apartment.

"I like animals. I lived on a ranch before, um, before my parents were killed." I take a gulp of my coffee, nervous. Maybe I shouldn't have said that. But I want to tell him. God, I want to tell him everything about me and ask him a million questions about him. I'm just so afraid he'll send me back to my uncle if I do.

His eyes find mine, his expression full of shock. "Killed? Your parents are dead?"

"They were murdered when I was seven," I whisper, and then I reach deep for a little courage and share a little more. "Sometimes, I forget what it was like to have a mom and dad who loved me. I remember bits and pieces, little flashes that feel almost as if they belong to someone else. I *know* my parents loved me. I just...don't remember exactly what that feels like anymore."

"Jesus. I'm so sorry," Shep murmurs, tugging me closer to him. He wraps his arms around me, enfolding me in his strong embrace. His lips touch my forehead, resting there for a moment. "I grew up in foster care. Until I joined the Navy, I didn't know what family meant."

"Being an orphan sucks."

"Yeah, it does."

I let him hold me, trying to absorb every second of it. He doesn't push for more about what happened to my parents or my life after they died. He simply holds me, satisfied with the little piece of my past that I shared freely. I think he meant what he said in the gym. He's not going anywhere.

Another piece of my heart lights up, branded with his name.

"I want you to stay here with me."

"I have to work," I say, regretfully. I'd rather stay here too, with his arms around me and his heart beating like my favorite song against my ear.

"No." He tips my chin up with a fingertip until our eyes meet. He's smiling, his expression so warm and gentle. "I don't mean right now. I mean I want you to move in here."

"I can't sleep with you," I blurt, shocked. "We haven't even been on a date yet. It's against the rules."

His smile grows bigger. "There are rules?"

"Yes. Milan says you're supposed to go on at least three dates before you do...sex things," I mumble, my cheeks heating. I'm not convinced she knows what she's talking about. She reads a lot, but she's never dated either. She's a virgin like me, only less sheltered. Her dad never has time for her. He tries to make it up to her by buying her things and sending her on lavish trips.

"Milan?"

"My best friend."

"Well, little lamb," Shep says, his deep voice pitched low so it grinds against something deep inside me, that same pleasure center that clenches and heats when he looks at me like he's hungry. "I hate to break your rules, but if you keep being this cute, we aren't going to make it to three dates."

My stomach sinks.

He must see it on my face because he curses. "That didn't come out right. I meant I'll be fucking you over every suitable surface long before three dates. The adorable shit you do keeps my dick hard."

"Shep," I whisper, my stomach clenching this time. And, oh, I like that way better than the sinking feeling. I'm not sure if I should like it when he says things like that to me or not. No one has ever spoken to me the way he does. But I love his honesty so much.

"It's true." He shrugs. "But just so we're clear, I'm not offering you a place to stay to get you in my bed. I'm offering because a motel is no place for you to live. The Witherbees are good people, but they're old. It's hard to keep a place like the Meadowlark safe. Besides, you need more space. You weren't designed to be cramped into a motel room."

He's not wrong, but.... "You've already done so much for me. I don't want to invade your personal space too." Okay, that's a lie. I do want to invade his personal space. But I can't tell him that, can I?

"Then we have a problem," he says, lips pursed and eyes narrowed.

"We do?"

He nods, taking my coffee mug and twisting to set it on the table behind the couch. Once it's out of the way, he pulls me flush against his body. "A big problem. Because that's not going to work for me."

"Oh." I lick my lips, shivering at the look in his eyes. They're so dark.

"Not having you in my personal space is driving me up the fucking wall," he growls, his hand slipping from my waist to my ass. He grips it hard, trying to pull me closer. I can't get any closer though, not without fusing our bodies into one.

I can't stop the little whimper that escapes my lips, either.

He hears it, and his eyes light up. Lord, he's beautiful.

"I want to kiss you every minute of the day, Ainsley."

"I...want that too," I whisper, my heart beating so loud I'm surprised he can't hear it. I've never been particularly brave. Until the day I ran away, I always just let Uncle Justice have his way. I never fought for what I wanted or asked for very much. But Shep makes me want to be brave. He makes me want to wriggle out of my shell and explore...everything.

"Shep? Can you kiss me now?" I plead, not letting the coward in me win this time. "Please?"

"Hell yes," he growls, and then his lips are on mine.

Unlike last night, this kiss isn't soft or sweet or simple. He thrusts his free hand into my hair, tilts my head back, and consumes me. His tongue touches my bottom lip, setting my soul on fire with bliss. I moan his name, and then he's licking into my mouth like he might die if he doesn't taste every part of me right this minute.

I wrap myself around him, practically climbing his body to get closer to him. He helps boost me up, moving me as if it's the easiest thing in the world. My back hits the wall a second later, my legs wrapping around his waist.

He's hard. Incredibly so.

I go up in flames. *Whoosh*!

"Shep," I moan, writhing as his erection settles against my center. His sweats and my leggings aren't much of a barrier. I can feel him against my clit. My entire body pulses with pleasure I've never felt before.

This, I realize, *this* is what's been missing since I got here. Him. This. His hands on my body and his lips on mine. This is why I can't get myself off anymore. I need him.

"Fuck," he groans, pulling my bottom lip between his teeth so it stings and throbs against my clit. "Work those hips and grind that juicy cunt all over me."

Then and only then do I realize that I'm doing exactly what he just said: gripping his shoulders tight to give me leverage so I can grind against his erection. I sob, unable to stop myself from chasing the pleasure he's giving me. It feels so good, and I've needed this so damn badly since I met him. I think I've needed him for longer than that.

He buries his face in my throat, licking and biting me there. It stings, making my clit throb. I feel everything there. Every little shift of his hips. The way his hands run all over my ass before he thrusts them into my leggings to grip my bare skin in his hands. The sound of his feral growl when he does it.

"Shep," I gasp as my clit begins to throb. "I'm going to...I'm going..."

"Ah, shit, lamb. You going to come for me now?" he asks, his voice a dark scrap of sound that sets my blood on fire. "Do it, baby girl. Let me see how good you look when you're screaming my name."

I don't scream it, but it's close. His name bubbles up from some deep-down place, erupting in a loud cry of ecstasy as his erection hits my clit just right and my entire body ignites. I shatter over and over, writhing all over him as the waves toss me around like a buoy.

He runs his hands all over me, keeping the fire inside burning until I slump against him, dragging air into my starving lungs in greedy gulps. And then he just holds me, pressing kisses to my crown again and again.

"We're going to get your shit today," he says.

"Okay," I whisper.

His relieved sigh lets me know he wants this as much as I do.

Chapter Five

"I need a favor."

"What's up?" Knight asks, looking up from the tattoo he's sketching out at his booth. He's got his long hair pulled back out of his face and his sleeves rolled up, showing off the ink on his arms.

"Ainsley's parents were murdered when she was a kid," I state, keeping my voice pitched low. I'm not worried about any of my Brothers overhearing, but Wild's working on a cager. Several others are hanging around. This place stays busy, and I don't want Ainsley's past leaking.

I was not prepared for her to tell me this morning that her parents were murdered when she was a little girl. It changed things. As much as I want her to trust me with her story, I need to know for sure that she's safe. Asking Knight to look into it is my compromise. He can tell me if she's safe. I can wait to hear the full story from her when she's ready to talk.

She probably won't be thrilled with me when she finds out I asked him to look, but I promised her no one would hurt her. The fact that her parents were murdered, coupled with the fact that she's been sheltered so close worries the fuck out of me. For my own peace of mind, I gotta have someone look into it.

"Damn," Knight says, shaking his head. "What do you need, brother?"

"I need to know she's safe," I murmur, grateful for the millionth time for the family I have here. My Brothers don't ask for explanations or justification. They just show up, ready to help. That sense of loyalty, that brotherhood, *that's* what this MC is about. We're family. No one rides alone.

"I'll hit up my sources," Knight says without hesitation, "see what I can dig up for you. You think there's going to be trouble?"

"Not sure," I admit. My gut is telling me someone is looking for her, but I don't know who. I don't know if they mean her harm. All I know is that she's mine to protect and I'll go to fucking war before I let anyone take her from here.

"You going to be willing to give her up if there is?"

"Nope."

"Figured you'd say that." Knight grins at me, amused. As much shit as I gave him over his ol' lady, he deserves to give it right back to me. Surprisingly, he doesn't. "It's a helluva ride, isn't it?"

"Yeah, it is," I say. Falling in love was not on my agenda. Don't get me wrong, I've hoped it was in the cards for me. But no one ever touched me in that way, made me want to fall until I set eyes on Ainsley. All it took was one look, and I was hers. She's mine.

I'll do whatever I have to do to keep her.

"You got anything solid?" Knight asks.

"Her last name is Foster. She's nineteen, parents were killed when she was seven," I murmur. "They may have owned a cattle ranch."

"What are you thinking?"

"Honestly?" I expel a breath. "My gut says someone is looking for her. Most likely family. She comes from money. Aside from not knowing much about the world, she's smart as hell, clearly educated. She's shy, sweet, but she's not fearful. She doesn't say much about her past, but she insists she's not in any danger."

"Won't hurt to know exactly what we're dealing with here," Knight says, his lips pursed. "If she does have family looking for her, it could get messy."

If anyone would know, he would. His ol' lady's uncle, our former Chief of Police, tried to hurt her. Knight took a bullet meant for her. Her uncle is gone now, handled like the rest of the trash in this town.

I still don't trust the cops here. Don't care who they bring in to straighten the place up. If Ainsley has family with money looking for her, I don't trust anyone but my Brothers to have my back and ensure she's able to stay right where she is. Money talks, especially to men with no morals or integrity.

"I'll see what I can find for you. Give me a day or two."

"Thanks, brother." I give him a fist bump and then turn to head out. I need to grab lunch for Ainsley, otherwise, I know she won't eat anything but a banana. She works her ass off. I don't know if she's worried I'll fire her if she takes it easy or if she just genuinely enjoys being busy, but the only time I can get her to take a break is when I distract her. Which I do frequently because I love talking to her.

Knowing she'll be in my bed tonight hasn't settled me any. Watching her come for me this morning was, hands down, the best experience of my life. I'm trying like hell not to rush her, but I want her naked in my bed so badly it's not even funny.

"You going to be calling us to Church soon?" Knight calls before I can walk away.

"Soon as I can make it happen," I mutter, striding toward the door.

His laughter floats after me.

"Shep."

I glance up from the counter in Rooster's where I'm waiting for our lunch to be boxed up, and curse when my gaze lands on Slate heading in my direction. He's the last person I expected to see today. I figured he'd avoid me until I hunted him down to have this conversation.

"Got a minute?" he asks, stopping in front of me. His expression is full of determination, his green eyes locked on me. A little guilt flickers there too.

"Yeah," I mutter, knowing I need to take care of this shit now. It'll save me from running all over town trying to track him down later. I catch Rooster's eye and jerk my head in a nod, letting him know I'm stepping out.

He nods back.

I turn on my heel and stride toward the door, Slate following behind me.

It's sunny out, warmer than usual for this time of year. Valor isn't large, but there are a few people out and about. A couple of teachers are chatting halfway down the street. Old Man Tiller's pickup is headed toward the hardware store at a slow crawl. His truck is older than Jesus.

I spin to face Slate, my jaw clenched. He's got his hands shoved into his pockets, his messy hair pulled back from his face. He's still young, just got back from his first tour with his SEAL team a few months ago. It doesn't excuse him for touching Ainsley last night.

There are rules. Even the sweet butts who hang around are treated with respect. If they aren't interested, you move the fuck along. You don't ever fucking touch a Brother's ol' lady without permission. I don't care if it was his hand on her face. He crossed a line. And he scared her in the process. I think I'm more pissed about that than about the fact that he put his hand on her.

"I fucked up," he blurts before I can say anything. "I was drunk and acted like an asshole. I didn't realize she was yours or I would have kept my hands to myself."

"You drink often?"

"Too much, maybe," he says, not lying about it. There are shadows in his eyes, the kind I'm all too familiar with. "Won't be doing it anymore."

"Good," I grunt. There are shadows in his eyes, the kind I'm all too familiar with. A lot of men who go to war come back and hit the bottle, trying to drown out the shit they dealt with overseas. It never ends well. I know from experience.

When I got back from my first tour, I hit the bottle nightly and woke up feeling like shit every day. I knew if I didn't put it down, eventually, it'd put me down. I walked away then and there and haven't picked up a bottle since.

"You need to talk to someone about what you did over there, you find me or one of the Brothers. You don't drown it in a sea of alcohol and bad decisions, you hear me?"

"Yeah, I hear you," he says. Another shadow crosses his expression. "Patriot reamed me last night. Pres. did first thing this morning. Figured I owed it to you to let you have your say too."

"Appreciate that," I mutter, impressed. "I planned on hunting you down later today."

He nods like he suspected as much.

We stand there for a long moment, staring at each other. It takes a hell of a man to admit he fucked up and try to make it right. Part of me still wants to break his jaw for touching her, for scaring her. Seeing that look in her eyes gutted me. Knowing what I know now, that her parents were murdered, I can't help but wonder if she's been sheltered for so long because she was hurt or kidnapped. I've had a thousand scenarios running through my head all day. Not knowing is going to eat me alive.

"I find out you've been anywhere near her, we're going to have a big fucking problem," I tell Slate. "She's mine. You don't touch her. You don't look at her. You don't step foot inside my gym while she's there. We clear?"

"We're clear."

"If I find out you're causing problems with any other women, Pres. and I will be having a conversation about you, and it won't end well for you. I'll make sure you aren't patched in. That shit doesn't fly around here," I growl at him.

"Understood." He takes a breath. "I saw her expression when I touched her. I know I scared her, getting all up in her space like an asshole. Would you tell her that I'm sorry?"

"I'll tell her," I mutter.

"Thanks." He tilts his head to the side, studying me. "Are we cool?"

I watch him for a minute, trying to decide if he's going to be a problem in the future. He's young, but he's not a bad guy. He's always been solid. If he lays off the drinking, I think he'll be straight.

"Don't fucking go near her and stop drinking so much, and we'll be cool," I mutter, letting it go for now. If he fucks up again or keeps drinking heavily, we'll deal with it then. But for now, I'll keep an eye on him. If we need to have another discussion like this, we'll be having it with Bullet. I wasn't playing about that. We've had one too many Prospects cross lines lately.

He sighs, his relief palpable. "Thanks, Shep."

I jerk my chin in a nod and then head back inside to grab Ainsley's lunch.

Chapter Six

"What do you think?" I ask, leaning up against the doorjamb as Ainsley wanders around my bedroom. There isn't much to see. Aside from the king-sized bed, a dresser, and the nightstands, the only other things in the room are a small television and the clothes hanging in the closet. I've never needed much. Growing up in foster care, I never had a whole lot. But if she needs something, wants to change something, she has free rein. I want her to be comfortable here. Happy.

She's been so quiet since we picked up her stuff from the Meadowlark. Actually, she's been quiet most of the day. I'm not sure if she's regretting what happened this morning, if she's just nervous, or what. It's making me anxious as hell though.

"Ainsley?"

"I lived with my uncle," she says.

I freeze, barely even breathing.

"I was always surrounded by people, but I never felt like I fit," she whispers, turning to face me. Her bottom lip is stuck firmly between her teeth, her blue eyes wide. "I feel like I fit here."

"You do fit here."

Her gaze roves over my face, searching for something. She swallows hard. "I'm afraid you might change your mind if I tell you about my life."

I push off the door, striding across the room toward her. She tilts her head back to look at me when I stop in front of her. The worry in her eyes is plain as day. So is the hope. She wants to trust me so badly. I can practically see it trying to burst free.

"Did you hurt anyone, lamb?"

She shakes her head no.

"Did you steal anything?"

"No."

"Kidnap anyone? Make meth or sell drugs?"

"No, of course not."

I reach for her hand, leaving her to decide if she wants to take it or not. She doesn't even think about it. She slips hers into mine, allowing me to pull her close. I reel her in, until we're pressed together in one long line.

"I want you to hear me, baby girl," I murmur, sliding my hand around to cup the back of her head. "Even if you had done those things, I wouldn't change my mind about you. There is nothing you could tell me about your past that would make me view you as anything less than the beautiful, brilliant woman you are."

She searches my face again. I know what she sees there. It's been there since day one, just waiting for her to recognize it. Waiting for her to be ready to see it, to feel it. The second she does, the last little glimmer of doubt in her eyes winks out. Her walls tumble down. And I know...she's finally mine.

"My parents were killed because my dad and my uncle put a man out of business," she says. "After he shot my dad, my mom hid me in a closet and then ran, trying to draw him away from me. I don't remember very much of it, but my uncle blames himself."

Jesus. No one, least of all someone like her, should have to go through something that goddamn tragic. She was just a little girl, a baby.

"He's been afraid my whole life that something like that would happen again and I wouldn't survive it this time," she continues, talking softly. "I had guards everywhere I went. No one was allowed to get too close. All the girls at school except for one avoided me. I've lived my entire life in this perfect little cage, able to look out at the world, but never to really experience it."

"Jesus," I whisper, wrapping my arms around her in a tight hug.

"A couple months ago, I overheard him talking about sending me somewhere. He called it a safe place, but it would have been another pretty cage." Her voice shakes, her tears dampening my skin where she's got her face pressed to my throat. "I couldn't do it anymore, Shep. If I had to spend another minute living that way, I would have lost my mind. So I made a plan to get out and I just...ran."

"Is he looking for you?"

"Probably," she whispers, pulling back to look at me. "I called him once from the road to let him know that I was safe. I left my phone behind. I haven't used my credit cards. I didn't even bring my car. Milan gave me hers so he couldn't track me. I love my uncle, but I don't want to go back."

"You're not going back, Ainsley," I promise, heat in my voice. I wipe her tears, trying to be gentle. I don't care what it takes or what I have to do, I won't let her uncle take her from me. If she needs someone to keep her safe from his enemies, it'll be me and my Brothers.

"I want to stay here, with you." Her cheeks heat, her teeth sinking into her lip again. "I mean...um, you don't have to give up your room for me. I can sleep on the couch until I can afford a place. But I want to stay in Valor."

I stare at her for a minute and then shake my head and chuckle. Of course she doesn't realize I want her in my bed with me. She really is a little lamb, lost in the great big world.

"I was kinda hoping you'd stay in here with me," I murmur, gently removing her lip from between her teeth. And then I run my finger over it, watching the way those bright eyes darken to a stormy blue.

"What if I steal all the covers? Oh my gosh. What if I *snore*?" she asks, sounding horrified by the prospect.

She's so fucking cute. My heart fills with pride for her, with gratitude for her. With empathy for her uncle, and regret for her. She wasn't made for a cage. She was made to live, to light this world up like the shining star she is.

"I'll never tell a soul," I swear, fighting a smile. "And we don't have to do anything but cuddle until you're ready for more. I won't rush you."

Her lip goes between her teeth again before she seems to catch herself doing it and lets it go. The color in her cheeks deepens. "What if I want to do...more than cuddle?"

"Yeah?" I ask, my dick stirring at the thought. "You want to come again?"

She bobs her head, her breathing growing choppy, her eyes darker. "I want..."

"What?" I whisper, turning her around in front of me, and then pulling her into my arms so I'm plastered to her back. My dick settles against her lower back. I place my lips against the side of her neck.

She melts against me, practically purring.

"Tell me what you want, Ainsley. You can have anything."

"I want to touch you."

"You want to make me come?" Just hearing her say she wants to touch me has me ready to blow right now. The thought of feeling that perfect little hand on my body, on my cock... God yeah, she can touch me. I need this girl to claim me as badly as I need to claim her.

"Yes," she moans.

"You want to feel me inside you, baby girl?"

"Shep," she whimpers, and I know I've got it right, know that's what she's after.

I'm not telling her no. Hell no, I'm not. I've been jacking my cock to fantasies of being inside her since day one. If I have my way, she'll be good and pregnant, wearing my ring and my patch, by the time her uncle comes looking for her.

I cup her tits. They're magnificent, more than a handful. Her nipples are hard points against my palms. I pinch them. Cum leaks into my boxers when she cries out, arching her back to get closer. That sweet voice is heaven-sent.

"You can touch me anytime," I murmur, flicking my tongue against the shell of her ear. "But I get to play with you first, lamb. I've been dying to put my mouth all over this body for two weeks. You going to let me do it?"

"Yes," she moans, her head lolling on my shoulder. "Please."

"I'm going to suck those little nipples until you're squirming, and then I'm eating your cunt, Ainsley," I growl, wanting her to know exactly what's going to happen. She's not experienced. I don't want anything I do to shock her. "You're going to come for me with my tongue buried inside you the first time."

"F-f-first time?"

"Yeah, the first time. I'll be nine deep the second and third time." And then I plan to cuddle the fuck out of her while she sleeps. In the morning, I'll eat her for breakfast, and then take her out like I planned. And then I'll figure out what to do about her uncle. She needs to reconcile with him. I know she won't be truly at ease until she does. I don't want guilt eating away at her.

"Shep!" she cries, trembling. "Please. Please."

Her sweet plea is all the answer I need.

I sweep her up into my arms, carrying her bridal style the few short feet to the bed. She wraps her arms around my neck like she's afraid I'm going to drop her. That won't happen. She's the best thing I've ever lifted. She's priceless, precious, a true treasure.

I've been prepared for weeks to hate whoever she was running from. Instead, I find myself...understanding. Survivor's guilt is a hell of a thing. I've been there, felt that. I'm not saying her uncle was right for putting her in a bubble like he did. But part of me is grateful as hell he cared enough to want to keep her safe.

This world can be ugly, full of terrible people who do terrible things. She's had enough of that in her life. Her uncle didn't go about protecting her the right way, but I can't be mad at the man for wanting to do it, for recognizing that she deserves to be protected.

Seeing her laid out in my bed, chafing her thighs together and whimpering my name, I know beyond a shadow of a doubt that there's no limit to the things I'd do for her. Shit. Look at me. I've been razzing my Brothers for weeks about their ol' ladies.

I would be the last one to fall. Like a goddamn meteor plummeting to earth.

I pull my shirt off over my head and then lean down to kiss her stomach where hers has ridden up. And then her tits. Her shoulder and her round cheek. My mouth touches the corner of hers. Her soft breath touches mine.

"I love you, Ainsley."

Her eyes pop open.

"Thought you should know that before I make love to you." I'm actually nervous. Soft and sweet...I'm not sure I know how to be that when I'm so amped up I'm ready to explode. But regardless of how this goes down, I *will* be making love to her. I feel nothing but complete adoration for this amazing girl.

"Shep," she whispers, wonder in those big blue eyes. Peace and bliss too. "I love you."

"Jesus," I breathe. It's a prayer of gratitude, of pride. Her words wash through me, lighting up those dark places. They wash away the stains on my soul, completely annihilate any chance of me ever letting her go. Maybe before she said those words, I would have let her go if it's what she really wanted, if it made her happy. Now though? Nu-uh.

I'll follow her to the ends of the earth. I'm her willing slave, her most ardent devotee.

I press my mouth to hers, trying to taste the shape of her words. Within seconds, I'm lost in her and the sweet sounds she makes when I touch my tongue to hers. She's tentative when she kisses me back, still learning. But she grows bolder, braver. Her tongue slips into my mouth, mimicking my moves. Her hands sink into my shoulders before sliding downward.

I groan at the feel of her palms against my bare skin. There's no way that should feel as good as it does. It's pure electricity crackling beneath her palms, hardening my cock until it presses against my zipper so tight the indentations it leaves behind may be as permanent as the ink on my back and ribcage.

I bite her lip, kiss each round cheek, and then work my way down. Even through her t-shirt and bra, her tits are incredible. I lick and bite her, teasing us both. I'm not sure which of us likes it more. She moans my name, writhing beneath me.

I kiss down her ribcage and belly, lifting her shirt to kiss a trail upward. Her stomach is round, her skin almost translucent. Her flesh pebbles beneath my eager mouth, and I love seeing it. Love knowing she's as affected by me as I am by her.

When I lift her shirt higher, she hesitates.

"You're so beautiful, Ainsley," I murmur, feathering kisses all along her ribcage. "Let me see you, baby girl. Let me love you."

"Shep," she whispers. Her hesitation melts away, her arms going up over her head.

I pull her shirt off, helping to lift her halfway up. Her bra is simple pink with lace detailing across the top. Her tits practically spill out of it, pushed up high in the cups. She's even more beautiful than I expected, her skin flushed and soft.

"Damn," I whisper, running a fingertip between her breasts and then down to circle her belly button. The way she responds to my touch is fascinating to me. A trail of goosebumps follow in my wake, as if her skin is rising up in protest of me leaving it behind.

I press my lips to her shoulder and then the little indent of her collarbone.

"Oh," she moans, her back bowing when I kiss all over her cleavage.

I bite and suck, marking her skin. I shouldn't, but I do it anyway, leaving love bites on her like a brand. Anyone who gets too close will know she's mine, that she's taken. That I've had my mouth all over her, pleasuring her. Shit. It's her mouth now. My fingers and cock too. Property of Ainsley, sweetest lamb ever created.

Cum spills into my boxers, my stomach going concave as soon as I undo her bra and peel it away from her skin. Her nipples are hard pink pebbles, her tits round and high. I memorize her like this, topless, chest heaving, lips parted. I'll be pulling this memory out and fucking my hand to it for years, whenever I can't slide between those thick thighs and ride her.

I lean down, tonguing her nipple and then pulling it into my mouth.

"Shep!" she cries in the sweetest voice, her nails digging into my upper back.

I torment her, teasing her mercilessly. Her nipples get harder, turn red.

"Please, please," she pleads, pulling at the short strands of my hair, pushing at my shoulders. She's an eager little thing, trying to move me where she needs me to go. I can't wait for the day she realizes how much power she holds here. She's going to use it against me, make me give her what she wants. I will, gladly.

I kiss down her belly again, nipping her while I work her leggings down. Her panties match her bra. They're soft pink, so wet I can see her bare lips clinging to them. She smells like vanilla sin, all sugar and sweet and sex.

"Don't hide from me, baby girl," I croon, tugging her hands aside when she tries to cover herself with them. My eyes seek hers out. "Never hide this beautiful body from me. It brings me nothing but pleasure."

"I've never..."

"I know."

She exhales a breath and nods, giving me permission to continue. She lifts her hips, letting me pull her leggings and panties off. I gently pry her legs apart, and then growl at the sight of her bare cunt. Jesus. I can't believe this is all mine. Don't know what I did right in my life, but if this is my reward, I'll do it a thousand times over.

"You've got the prettiest little pussy, Ainsley," I murmur, wedging my body between her legs. They part around me, her hard clit peeping out from between the lips of her pussy. And fuck. I'm never going to get another thing done. I'm going to spend every waking moment right here between her legs, worshiping.

I've gone without for years. Sweet butts, strippers, the women who come into my gym...none of them ever tempted me. When my cock got hard, I handled it myself. But this pussy right here? It's not a mere temptation. It's the goddamn holy grail.

And it's mine.

I kiss all over her thighs, my mouth watering at the smell of her, at the little taste of her juices against her skin. She's ambrosia, the sweetest thing to ever cross my lips. I run my lips all over her mound, letting her get used to having me here. She's shy and sweet, gasping my name. She doesn't try to hide from me anymore.

I press my tongue against her slit, licking her from the bottom to the top.

"Oh!" she cries out, her legs coming together and then flying apart.

If heaven is real, this is it right here. She's perfect in a way that defies description. Jesus. I dig my hands into the comforter, fighting the urge to attack her cunt like a rabid dog. She lifts her hips off the bed trying to get closer, and I lose the fight.

The sound of the comforter ripping, her scream, and my growl crash together, all hitting my ears at the same time. I bury my face in her cunt, grab her round ass and pull her closer. She's so fucking good. I can taste the virginity on her, that cherry taunting me.

Ainsley isn't quiet in bed. She isn't shy and timid. She screams the roof down as I eat her. She claws and scratches, babbling like she can't stop herself.

Her hips roll in my hands as she tries to ride my face from beneath me, tries to get closer and take more.

I suck her clit into my mouth, grinding my chin against her pussy. Her legs tighten around my head, her ass coming completely off the bed. I growl, releasing one plump cheek to thrust my finger into her. She's tight as hell but so wet I slip in easy.

"Shep!" she shouts. "Oh god. Oh god. Oh god."

Here, like this, with her taste on my tongue and my finger in her little fuckhole, I feel like a god. I'm invincible. And she's so fucking *mine*. I replace my finger with my tongue, fucking her with it. She shouts my name again, wailing it into the room.

She does it again when I spread her cheeks and lick her there too. Her sobs rebound off the high ceiling, floating through the room like music. I eat her asshole, pressing my tongue deep, claiming that little part of her as mine too. She loves it, the dirty little lamb.

One more lick and she cracks. If any of my Brothers are downstairs, they hear her coming and screaming and *coming*. Jesus. She comes so hard she squirts. I roar like a lion as soon as I feel it, attack her like a wild animal.

She writhes beneath me, practically convulsing her way through it. I don't let up until I've worked every last bit out of her, claimed every last drop of her cream. Her body falls limp beneath me. I pry myself from between her legs, pressing a last kiss to her swollen clit.

She startles, moaning.

I make quick work of my sweats and boxers, throwing them over the side of the bed. I should probably be ashamed of how wet they are with my cum. I'm not. Nothing has ever gotten me as hot as this perfect little lamb or made me ache as badly as she does.

Her dazed eyes meet mine. Her pupils are so dilated, she looks like she's high enough to levitate. I memorize her like this too, legs spread wide, hands limp at her side, wrung out. Beautiful. So fucking beautiful.

"You still want to touch me?" I ask.

"Yes."

I move closer to her, my cock bobbing like he's dying for the attention.

Her gaze drifts over me.

"I like your tattoo," she says, all shy and sweet, like I didn't just have my mouth all over her.

"Yeah?" I smile as her eyes drop lower.

She swallows hard, her eyes locked on my cock.

"I'll go slow," I murmur, trying to ease her mind. Fuck, I hope I can keep that promise. I want in her so badly, I'm a little afraid I'll screw it up. No. No, I won't. The certainty bubbles up from some deep-down place, settling my nerves. She was made for me to love her, to protect her. I won't mess that up.

"You're beautiful everywhere, Shep," she says.

"You're the beautiful one." I settle next to her, wrapping my fist around my cock. She keeps being so fucking cute, I won't last long enough to make it inside her. "Touch me, baby girl. Make me yours."

The little rebel peeks out from those eyes again, bolder than before.

"You're already mine."

"Fuck yeah," I growl, liking the way that sounds a whole hell of a lot.

She reaches out, running her hand down my abs. They clench beneath her palm. Her eyes flare with heat, with satisfaction. I like seeing it there.

I like seeing her hand on my cock just as much.

"Fuck," I grit out, cum spilling out onto her hand when she wraps it around me. Her fingers barely fit around my shaft. Her hand is so soft. She looks damn good with it on me.

"You're so hard," she whispers. "So hot." Her eyes flit upward, seeking out mine. "I want to do what you did to me."

"Jesus," I groan. "You're trying to kill me, aren't you?"

"No, I..." She blushes. "I want to taste you. I like the thought."

"Taste me, baby girl. Suck me. I'm yours, do what you will." I'm not sure if I'm granting permission or begging here. I'm not sure it matters either way.

She turns onto her side, propping herself up on one elbow. I grit my teeth and clench my hands, trying to stay still and let her do this her way. It's hard though, giving up control. Guys like me...we thrive on that shit, on being the ones who call the shots. I can't even lie though, being at this girl's mercy is sexy as fuck.

She strokes her hand up and down my length, exploring, playing. Her grip is loose, like she's afraid she's going to hurt me.

"Harder," I demand, rocking my hips forward.

She squeezes me tighter.

"God yeah," I groan.

She takes her time, torturing me without even realizing she's doing it. I love the look on her face though. She's completely focused on what she's doing. Excitement flashes in her eyes. She leans forward.

I nearly cum all over her when her lips touch the head of my cock. Her tongue follows, running over the broad head, licking up my cum.

"Fuck," I choke out, clinging to composure by the skin of my teeth.

She pauses for a minute, trying to decide if she likes the way I taste. I guess so because she licks me again like I'm a fucking lollipop. It's the best kind of torture.

"Put me in your mouth, Ainsley. Suck me."

I don't have to tell her twice. She tips her head forward. Her warm mouth surrounds the head of my cock. It's obvious she doesn't know what she's doing, but that only seems to make me hotter.

Shit. Who am I kidding?

Knowing I'm the first man who has ever touched her, that my cock will be the only one she ever takes into that hot little mouth...there's nothing I don't love about that.

She moans, and I damn near lose it right there.

"You're done," I growl, pulling back.

Her eyes narrow on me, that attitude of hers coming out to play. "I wasn't done," she argues, reaching for my dick again. "I want to taste you again."

"You want me coming in your mouth? Because if you put it on me again, that's what's going to happen, Ainsley. I'll be coming down your pretty throat instead of breeding that cunt."

"B-breeding?" Her wide eyes meet mine.

"I'm not wearing a rubber. When I'm in you, I'll be bare."

"You want to get me pregnant," she says, scrutinizing my expression.

It's not really a question, but I answer it anyway.

"I need it so fucking badly I'm ready to beg," I say, telling her nothing but the truth. "Seeing you with that little girl on Monday nearly killed me."

"I thought about it then," she admits. "About what it would be like to have a little boy who looks like you or a little girl who follows you around all the time." A smile twists at her lips before slipping. "I didn't think I could have it."

"You thought wrong."

I flip her onto her back and move between her legs again, seaming my body to hers, pressing her down into the bed beneath me. I keep most of my weight off her, just let her feel me there. She shivers, letting me know she likes it.

"You can have anything you want. Babies," I whisper, running my lips along the side of her face. "A ring. Your farmhouse. Anything."

"Shep." She turns her face toward mine, silently demanding a kiss.

I give it to her. For long moments, we just kiss. I swear, I could kiss her for days and not grow tired of it. She tastes herself on me and moans. I roll my hips so my cock nudges her clit.

"Shep," she moans into my mouth.

We grind and kiss and touch, getting lost in one another. Her cunt grows wetter, her thighs becoming slick with her juices. They soak my cock. My balls draw up, aching. I can't breathe through the desire churning through me.

I need in her before I lose my mind. I line myself up at her entrance.

"Shh," I croon when she tenses. "It's all right, lamb. I won't hurt you. Do you want me to stop?"

"No. Don't stop."

There is no way to make this easier for her. My cock is a monster and she's never had anything more than my finger inside her. I try to take it slow though, pushing forward little by little.

As soon as her heat surrounds the head of my cock, my eyes threaten to roll back in my head. Fuck. She's tight and hot, choking my cock.

"Shep," she whimpers in pain. The sound breaks my heart. So do the tears welling in her eyes.

"I'm sorry, lamb," I murmur, kissing them away. And then I snap my hips forward, trying to get her through the worst of it.

She cries out as I tear through her hymen. And I feel like an asshole for being in heaven while she's got tears dripping down her cheeks. But god, she feels good.

"Breathe for me, Ainsley," I whisper, pushing through the need to move, pushing it aside. It's hard as hell, but she comes first. In all things. In all ways. Always. "Breathe, baby girl. You're breaking my heart."

"I'm sorry," she sobs, scoring her nails down my back. "It hurts. It feels so good. *God*, Shep."

Triumph, possession, *something* rushes through me, settling into place. It lights me up, tying me to her with invisible threads no one can break or shatter or remove. For the rest of my life and whatever comes next...I'm hers, the blade at her back, the wall standing in front of her, her home.

"I love you," I whisper, kissing all over her face, her lips and cheeks and eyes. "God, Ainsley. Never knew love until you, baby girl. I didn't know it'd be this fucking perfect."

"M-me either." She sniffles. "I love you. I love you so much. Please don't let him take me away from you."

"Never," I vow, kissing her on the lips. I slide out an inch and then press forward, tentative, desperate. God, I need to move something fierce. I need to fuck her, claim her, remind her that she's mine and nothing can change that.

"Oh," she moans.

The vise around my heart loosens.

I rock my hips again.

When she moans a second time, I exhale a relieved breath...and then I let go. There is no going slow now, no being gentle. I fuck her hard, pounding into her like my life depends on it. Shit. Maybe it does. Because if I don't feel her coming on me soon, I'm going to lose it.

Her loud cries let me know she's right there with me. She claws my back, writhing beneath me. She works her hips like she's trying to ride me from below. She's a horny little virgin, fucking me like she can't stop.

"Shep, Shep," she gasps. "It feels s-so good!"

I chuckle through a groan.

"Please don't stop. Never s-s-stop. You feel l-like heaven on top of me, inside of me. Why does it feel so *good?*" she sobs.

"You keep talking, you won't be able to walk straight tomorrow, Ainsley," I growl, yanking her leg up higher, opening her up to me. I capture her nipple between my teeth, delivering a sharp little bite.

She wails my name, going off like a firecracker. She soaks my cock with her juices, thrashing beneath me as she comes hard and fast. Her cunt locks down on my dick hard enough to hurt.

I grit my teeth and go harder, deeper, fucking her through it.

She goes wild.

I pry myself off her and flip her over onto her stomach, yanking her hips up high. Her head flies back on a shout when I push into her again. I can't stop myself from wrapping her hair around my fist to pull her head back.

"Work those hips now, Ainsley," I growl against her lips. "Fuck me back."

She sobs into my mouth and gives me what I want. It takes her a minute to figure it out, but she does. She rocks backward, slamming herself onto my cock. It's too rough, too much for her first time.

"Easy, baby girl, easy," I murmur, not wanting her to hurt herself. I hold her hip in my hand, moving with her. She catches on quick, rocking in time to my thrusts. Once I'm sure she isn't going to hurt herself, I let go of her hip, running my hand all over her ass. It's so round, so sexy.

I reach around her, playing with her tits and then her clit. Her juices drip down my hand.

"Oh god," she moans when I press my thumb against her back entrance.

"You like that?" I ask.

She whimpers instead of answering me.

"I'm going to fuck you here one day, Ainsley," I murmur, kissing all over her upper back. "Every part of you will belong to me."

"Shep."

I play with her asshole, toying with her. I don't push my finger into her. As much as I want to do it, there's time for that later. Right now, I just want to love her, show her how good it's going to be between us. Already, it's better than anything I've ever experienced. She's utter perfection, so soft and sweet. So damn horny for it.

"You gotta come for me again," I mutter, pulling my hand away to play with her clit again. I can feel my orgasm building. It tingles at the base of my spine and deeper. My balls draw up, ready to blow.

I'm deeper this way, my cock right at her cervix, making it real easy to fill that womb full of my seed. I want her pregnant with my kid now.

Fuck taking it slow. Fuck all that bullshit. She and I are a done deal, permanent.

I pump into her a little harder, a little deeper, trying to get her there before I do. She sobs my name, her pussy fluttering around my cock. I press my thumb to her clit and jiggle it, sinking my teeth into her shoulder at the same time.

She goes off like fireworks. *Pop. Pop. Pop.*

My name breaks on her lips, her pussy locking down on my cock.

I roar her name as her orgasm rips my own from me, pulling it out of me like it's hers to command. Shit, I guess it is now, isn't it? Cum shoots up my cock, her pussy draining me dry. She writhes through her orgasm, whimpering in that sweet little voice that drives me so crazy. It's good.

God, it's so damn good.

I lose track of everything, my vision dimming, blood rushing in my ears.

We fall together, landing in a sweaty, sated heap of trembling limbs and sticky juices. Of bliss and love and all that incredible shit I never knew existed until she walked into my life. I'm still inside her, wrapped around her. We pant for breath, pulling air into our lungs as one.

I hold her close, my throat tight with emotion, my heart full. With her in my arms and my Brothers at my back...I've got everything I need.

"I love you, lamb," I whisper, pressing my lips to her shoulder.

"Shep," she whispers back. "My Shep."

Her Shep. I smile. Yeah, I like that.

Chapter Seven

"We're going to play poker?" I ask Shep, sticking close to his side as we approach the clubhouse on the outskirts of town. The club looks like a giant warehouse, surrounded by acres of land. There are houses further back on the property where several of the Brothers live. Like at Midnight Oil, a row of bikes is parked out front.

"No. We're going on a poker run," Shep says, chuckling.

"Oh. I don't know what that is, but I was kind of looking forward to kicking your butt."

"You can play poker?"

"My uncle taught me. He may have been a card shark in a past life."

"You saying you're good, Ainsley?"

"I learned fast. I *could* beat you."

Shep chuckles again, shaking his head. "It'll never happen."

"It might," I mutter, though I can't help but smile. I haven't been able to stop smiling since last night.

Telling him about my life was the right thing to do. I wrestled with my fears all day yesterday, feeling horrible. Keeping the truth from him, not trusting him with it, didn't feel right.

For once in my life, I get to decide what happens to me...and I didn't want my secrets standing like a mountain between us. Telling him about my life might have pushed him away, but not trusting him would have been worse, I think. It would have destroyed us before we ever had a chance. I didn't want that to happen. I didn't want him to feel like I was hiding this big thing from him when he's been nothing but amazing to me.

I still haven't told him exactly who my uncle is, but I *am* going to tell him. I don't want to spend the rest of my life hiding from Justice or looking over my shoulder. Sooner or later, I'm going to have to face him. But for now, I just want a few more days to just...be.

I want to fall asleep in Shep's arms and wake up to him eating me like I did this morning. I want to be young and in love and just *live*. And then I'll ask Shep to go with me to talk to my uncle. I'm not going back home, no matter what Uncle Justice says. I'm staying right here. I've never fought for anything in my life. But I'll fight for Shep, for *us*.

Shep stops walking halfway up the driveway. He turns toward me, pulling me into his arms. I snuggle up against his chest, my head resting against his heart. It thrums beneath my ear, strong and steady, just like him. His arms feel like heaven around me. I never knew how amazing being held like this could feel.

"Are you sure you're ready to do this?" he asks, his lips against my crown.

I know what he means, what he's asking. If I'm ready to let the whole world know that I'm his. Okay, maybe not the *whole* world...but definitely all the people in his world who matter to him. It's like meeting the family.

Maybe I should be nervous, but I'm not. I've never been *more* ready for something in my life. I want everyone to know that I chose Shep. That I will always choose him and all of them. I know I'm not their family yet, but I'm kind of hoping they'll want to keep me too.

"I'm ready," I promise Shep, tipping my head back to smile at him. "I want everyone to know I'm yours."

"Fuck," he growls, pride flaring bright in his cinnamon eyes.

His mouth slashes down over mine. He kisses me hard, flicking his tongue against my lips in a silent demand for entry. I give it to him, moaning at how thoroughly he claims my mouth. He kisses me like he's not capable of stopping himself. He touches me that way too.

Last night was indescribable. I was wrong. He wasn't rough...well, he wasn't *only* rough. He was sweet and soft and rough and dirty and perfect. I loved every second of what we did together.

He put me in the bathtub after, worried that I was going to be too sore to straddle his bike today. I'm not. I mean, I'm a little tender. But a couple of Tylenol knocked it right out this morning.

Mostly, I'm ready to do it again. He wouldn't let me get my hands on him this morning. Which really isn't fair since he ate me until I was babbling like a crazy person.

"Get a room!" one of his Brothers shouts.

Raucous laughter spills across the yard.

I freeze in Shep's arms.

"Fuck off!" he yells back, not even looking up. He tries to kiss me again as his Brothers catcall and toss playful insults and racy suggestions his way.

"They're all watching us," I whisper, my cheeks burning.

"Ignore them and kiss me."

"I can't. It's weird," I hiss at him.

"You're killing my ego here," he says. His chuckle lets me know he's just teasing. He brushes his lips against mine and then my forehead. "Come on. Let's go say hi."

"Wait," I whisper, grabbing onto his cut. "What if they ask me motorcycle questions?"

"They're not going to ask you motorcycle questions."

"They might. What if they're all, *Ainsley, which do you prefer, a Harley or a Ducati?* And then expect me to answer and I blurt out something like 'I prefer a mountain bike, Knight.' They'll never want to keep me then!"

"Breathe, lamb."

I faceplant into his chest, taking a deep breath. It doesn't help calm the butterflies suddenly fluttering in my stomach. I wasn't nervous until they all saw us kissing. What if I'm not good at it and they know?

"I'm scared," I whisper. "What if they hate me?"

"Hey, hey," he says, his voice soft. "Why do you think they'll hate you? What are you thinking?"

"I don't know! We had sex."

"Made love, Ainsley," he growls, which is way hotter than it should be. His cinnamon eyes scan across my face. "You worried they're going to change their minds about you now that we aren't pretending you don't belong to me?"

"Yes. No." I huff. "No. I'm just freaking out because they caught us making out. What if they're annoyed by it? I don't want them to not like me, Shep."

"Lamb," he whispers, shaking his head. His expression is soft and warm. He places his hands on my shoulders. "They'll like you."

"How do you know?"

"Because I know you, baby girl. It's impossible to know you and not love you."

"Shep." My whole body relaxes. His faith in me is absolute. It gives me courage.

"Do you trust me?"

"Yes," I whisper, a little awed at how much I trust him. When I decided to tell him the truth yesterday, I didn't know how much closer to him I would feel. But I *do* feel closer to him, like he's a part of me. He would never do anything to hurt me. Deep down, I think I knew that all along and was just afraid to let myself fall any harder for him.

"Then trust me when I say that no one is going to think badly of you because they caught us making out. It may be the first time, but I can promise you it won't be the last time," he says...which doesn't really help.

But I take a deep breath anyway and push down the fear, refusing to let it rule me. He wouldn't lie to me.

"I'm ready," I say a moment later.

"You sure?"

I nod.

"I love you, brave girl," he says, pressing his lips to mine in a sweet kiss.

And those three little words—*I love you*—settle me like nothing else. They give me the courage to slip my hand into his and let him turn me to face his Brothers. I recognize most of them...Knight, Rooster, Bullet, and Patriot are all standing at the bottom of the steps like a solid wall of muscle. They're all wearing matching grins.

"Hi," I whisper when we reach them.

"So you're with this one, huh?" Bullet asks me, jerking his head in Shep's direction.

"Yes, sir. Um, I hope that's okay."

He eyes me for a minute and then shakes his head, smiling. His green eyes are kind. "Yeah, I think that's going to be just fine."

Hearing it from the President of the club settles the rest of the butterflies in my stomach, allowing me to take a deep breath. I take a moment to peek up at the rest of the Brothers. They're all so alike and yet so incredibly different. They're big, most of them tattooed. They're all wearing their cuts. When I look at Knight, I notice him watching me.

He notices me noticing and gives me a nod.

"Come on," Shep murmurs, sliding his arm around my waist. "Let's get you inside, and then I need to talk to my Brothers for a minute, all right?"

"Okay."

The Brothers all file in with Patriot bringing up the rear. He's not quite a brother yet, but they all treat him like he's a full-fledged member of the club. Shep says he probably will be soon. That makes me happy for him. He's a good guy, and it's obvious how much everyone cares for him.

The club is not what I expected. Honestly, I'm not sure what I expected. But this place is neat and clean. There are pool tables set up in the main room, with tables and chairs scattered around. A few of the women are at a big table with a couple of the Brothers, chatting back and forth.

"Need to talk to you, brother," Knight says to Shep.

He jerks his chin in a nod and then leans down to me. "Will you be all right out here with Patriot for a few minutes?"

"Yes," I promise, tilting my face up to his. "I'll be fine."

He presses a kiss to my temple, grins at me, and then follows behind Knight to a room in the back. All the Brothers follow behind him, including the couple who were at the table with the women.

"Is everything okay?" I ask Patriot when Knight looks at me again before pulling the door closed behind Shep.

"It's all good," Patriot says. "Club business. You want to meet the other ol' ladies?"

I scrunch my nose up at the term, which makes him chuckle.

"It's not a bad word," he teases me.

"I know." Shep explained to me what it means. It's honestly kind of sweet. I saw the way he looked at me when he said it, the reverence in his eyes. He can call me whatever he wants to call me. He's mine and I'm his. That's all that really matters to me at the end of the day. The term still makes me want to giggle though.

Patriot leads me over to the other women, introducing me to those I don't know. There are fewer I don't know than I expected. I've met most of them in town, at the gym, or at Midnight Oil on Friday. Those I've already met smile at me and welcome me. Those I haven't are just as nice. It's an entirely different world than the one I grew up in, where everyone always maintained a polite distance and acted a little like they were afraid of me as much as they were of earning my uncle's ire.

There's none of that here. Within minutes, we're all chatting like old friends.

The mood shifts when the door to the back room opens. Shep strides out ahead of his Brothers. As soon as I spot him, I know something happened. He's tense, his expression harder than usual. My stomach sinks all the way into my shoes.

He heads right for me.

"Is everything okay?" I ask, suddenly nervous.

"Yeah," he murmurs, holding out a hand to me. "Come on."

"Where?"

"Bullet wants to talk to you."

I gulp, suddenly nervous all over again. But I slip my hand into Shep's, letting him pull me from the chair. He leads me past the room they were just in, cutting down the hallway. Bullet and Knight are at the far end. They see us coming and step into a doorway on the right.

"What's wrong, Shep?" I whisper.

"Everything is okay," he says, but I'm not even sure he believes it. He sounds worried. Or mad. I'm not sure. And I don't have time to figure it out because we're already ducking through the doorway behind Bullet and Knight. The room is a bedroom, but it's completely empty.

Bullet and Knight are standing in the center.

Shep pushes the door closed and then turns me around to face him.

"I don't want you to be mad when I tell you this," he murmurs, placing my hand on his chest. His cinnamon eyes meet mine, more serious than I've ever seen them.

"Okay," I whisper.

"Yesterday, before you told me about your uncle, I asked Knight to look into your past," he says. "After you told me about your parents, I needed to know that you were safe."

I process that, not sure how I feel about it. Guilty because he was worried about me. Sad that he thought he didn't have a choice but to look into it without telling me. Embarrassed that Knight knows about my life before Valor. Worried that Bullet is here to tell me that I can't stay. Terrified that he's going to send me back home and I'll never see Shep again.

"Is Justice Foster your uncle, baby girl?" Shep asks.

"I'm sorry I didn't tell you," I blurt, tears welling in my eyes as soon as he says my uncle's name. "I planned on telling you soon. I just wanted time with you before I told you about him." I turn to look at Bullet "If you don't want me here anymore, I'll leave. Just don't be mad at Shep. He didn't know."

"The hell you will," Shep growls, yanking me into his arms.

I collide with his broad chest, his arms encircling me like he intends to keep me right where I am, no matter who he has to fight to do it. And I love him so much for that, but I don't want him to fight his Brothers over me.

"You aren't going anywhere, Ainsley," Shep whispers into my hair, his voice hard, full of tension. I feel it in his body too, his muscles rigid, like he thinks he may have to use them at any moment to protect me.

"We aren't asking you to leave," Bullet says.

"You aren't?"

"Hell no," Shep growls.

"But..." I blink, confused. I really thought Bullet and Knight were here to tell me that I can't stay, that they don't want the kind of trouble Uncle Justice could cause them. "I'm confused."

"Your uncle is looking for you," Shep murmurs. "He reported you as missing."

"Oh no," I whisper, my heart sinking.

"He's offering a million-dollar reward for your safe return."

I blanche, shocked.

"Your friend, Milan. Did you know she was seeing your uncle, Ainsley?" Shep murmurs, his voice soft.

"She's seeing Justice?" I can tell by his expression that he's not joking. "Milan and Uncle Justice are together? Like *together* together?"

"They got married last week," he mutters.

"I... No," I say, shaking my head. "I had no idea." Neither of them ever said anything. I mean, I knew Milan thinks Justice is hot. She's commented on it before, but I didn't know they were together or that either of them even liked the other. Milan always aggravated him, challenged him. She said because he's a bossy bastard who has gotten too used to no one ever gainsaying him.

Her house is one of the few places I could go without causing a scene, so we hung out there all the time. My security guards were comfortable enough to leave us in the house alone so long as her dad wasn't home. That's how I managed to run away.

"Her car!" I say, my eyes going wide. "Shep, I have her car."

"I know." He stares at me for a moment. "We need to contact him, lamb. If he's got half the state looking for you, someone is going to recognize you sooner or later. I'd rather do this on our terms than have the cops trying to drag you away."

"The reward," I say. My stomach flutters, fear rushing through me in a flood. I fight it back, trying hard to contain it. A million-dollar reward is massive, especially if the cops in this town really are as bad as Shep says they are...and everything I've learned since I've been here leads me to believe he's not wrong. Knight was shot. Patriot was hurt. Others have been too. How much damage would they do for a million dollars? How many more people would they hurt?

"I'm not interested in the money, Ainsley," Shep growls, narrowing his eyes on me.

"Of course not," I promise. The thought never crossed my mind. I made my choice when I told him about my life yesterday. I trust him. I love him, unconditionally. Justice could offer him a billion dollars to give me up, and it'd just piss him off. "That's not what I was worried about."

"I believe she meant us," Bullet says, his tone dry.

"I didn't," I swear, turning to him. He doesn't look mad though. Honestly, he seems...amused, like he thinks it's hilarious I would worry they'd turn me in. But I've gotten to know these guys and everything Shep told me about them that first day is true. They're good guys, trustworthy. They care about each other and about this town. They may do bad things sometimes, but only when they don't have a choice.

"There are other people in town, people who could probably use that kind of money," I say quietly. "If my face is all over the news, it's only a matter of time until someone tells Justice I'm here." My gaze flits to Knight and then back to Bullet. "I don't want to make trouble for any of you."

"Which is why we're going to contact your uncle," Shep says, turning me with gentle hands to face him. "You gotta talk to him, baby girl. We won't let him take you if you don't want to go, but we need to sort this shit now."

"Promise you won't make me go back with him?"

Shep's eyes narrow. "When are you going to learn, lamb? You're mine. No one takes what belongs to me."

"We won't let him take you," Bullet agrees.

I take a deep breath and then nod.

"Then I guess we need to call my uncle."

Pride flares in Shep's cinnamon eyes.

"Hey, I murmur, practically leaping up from my chair when Shep, Bullet, and several of the Brothers emerge from the private room they use for Church, which I thought meant there was a preacher here. The Brothers cracked up. Shep had to explain what Church means. It's not my fault I didn't know! They've been in there for a while talking to Uncle Justice because Shep wanted to talk to him before deciding whether to take me to see him or not.

I'm worried as hell it didn't go well and there will end up being some war between him and Justice. If ever there were two men capable of raging a war over my future, it would be the two of them. They're a lot alike. They're both bossy and used to being obeyed. I want them to like each other, but I'm worried they'll hate each other. If Uncle Justice tried to threaten Shep, he probably didn't take it very well. He gets growly when it comes to me.

"Come here," he says, pulling me into his arms.

I burrow into him, resting my head against his chest. The steady thrum of his heart against my ear eases the worst of my anxiety. His scent washes through me, calming the furious churning of my stomach. No one has ever smelled better than Shep does. I didn't know home had a smell until I met him, but it does. My home smells like leather and sunshine.

"Are we going to see him?" I ask, ready to know what happens next. If I don't know soon, I might actually explode. All the uncertainty is a lot of stress. I don't think I realized just how stressful the last few weeks have been until I woke up in Shep's bed this morning, feeling at peace for the first time in...ever. I've never felt like I did this morning. I want the running and hiding to be over so badly so I can get back to reveling in that feeling.

"No."

"No?"

His Brothers and their ol' ladies murmur back and forth and then the front door opens. When the door closes again, silence falls in the main room. I guess everyone left to give us a little privacy.

"No?"

Shep sighs, tipping my chin up until our eyes meet. His run across my face, soft and full of concern. He's always worrying about me, checking on me. I love him so much for caring as much as he does. No one has ever loved me like he does or cared what I want as much as he does.

"He wants to come here, see shit for himself."

"Oh." I swallow hard. "Is that a good thing?"

"Don't know," Shep admits, frowning. "He's not what I expected."

"He's not a bad man," I whisper, knowing Shep doesn't trust him much. He's as protective as Uncle Justice is, but it's different with him. He wants me to live, not just exist. I think it bothers him that Justice hurt me by keeping me locked away.

"He's worried about you."

"I know," I whisper, feeling guilty. That wasn't what I wanted when I left. I just didn't think I had another choice. He never would have let me go on my own. I suggested going to the mall without security one day. I thought he was going to have a heart attack. "How mad is he?"

"He's not mad at you. He's worried," Shep murmurs. "He wants you to call him. I think you should, baby girl. It'll ease his mind." He runs his lips across my forehead, feathering my crown with kisses. "Yours too."

"Okay," I agree, relieved he thinks it's a good idea. That has to be a good sign...right?

"I told him that I'm marrying you."

I blink.

"Thought he should know," he says.

"How'd he take it?" I whisper, almost afraid to ask.

"He threatened to kill me if I put a ring on your finger before he gets here." Shep's lips curve into an amused smirk. "He didn't seem surprised when I told him I'd consider waiting."

"Shep," I whisper, partly exasperated because I know he's probably editing what he said to make it sound less bossy and rude than it was in reality, and partly swooning because I like how boldly he says I'm his. It's sexy as hell.

"We're getting married, lamb. I'll sign whatever the fuck he wants me to sign to protect your trust fund, but you're going to be my ol' lady, and it's going to be legal. He doesn't get a say in that." His eyes flash with heat, with fire. "And just so we're clear, regardless of whatever he wants me to sign, there will be no divorcing. There will be no other man for you. We're permanent."

"Good," I say, lifting up on my toes to kiss his jaw. "Because I don't ever want you to divorce me. I won't ever want anyone else. But I don't want you signing anything. My money is your money."

"Never," he growls, sinking his hands into my hips to yank me up against him. He kisses me hard, claiming my mouth again. His hands prowl all over my ass and then he curses. "I hate these fucking pants."

"Why? What's wrong with them?"

"They aren't your leggings."

I laugh against his lips. "You're the one who told me to wear jeans today."

"I'm an idiot. Clearly. You should only ever wear leggings or dresses." He kisses me again and then reluctantly pulls back. "I already agreed to sign whatever he wants me to sign. Your money is your money. We don't need it."

I frown at him.

"It's your money," he says, his voice firm.

"Fine," I huff. My parents left everything to me. I'm pretty sure Justice has been putting money into the account for me too. I don't know what's in it. I'd rather have my family back than all the money in the world. I think Shep knows it too because he kisses me again.

"Let's go call your uncle."

"Okay."

He smiles at me. "You're so sweet and cuddly after I kiss you."

"I like kissing you."

"Yeah?" His eyes heat and darken. "Call your uncle, and then I'll take you home and do more than kiss you."

"Shep," I moan, my entire body catching fire. And then I frown. "I thought we were going on a poker run?"

"We're going to skip it this time," he murmurs.

"Oh, but I want to go." The other ol' ladies explained the concept to me while the Brothers were in Church. Everyone gets a score sheet and has to pick up a card at each stop along the route. At the end, whoever has the best hand wins bragging rights. It sounds like a lot of fun.

"Your face is all over the news," he murmurs, his voice soft. "I think it's best if we hang back today. At least until shit with Justice is resolved and the reward is off the table."

"Oh." Disappointment filters through me. I love being on the back of his bike with him. It feels a little like flying, only better because I get to cuddle up to him at the same time.

"We'll go next time," he promises, reading my expression. "We have a whole lifetime to ride together, lamb."

"Okay," I agree, smiling at the thought of spending a lifetime exploring the world on the back of his Ducati. Nothing has ever sounded so much like heaven.

Chapter Eight

"More of your Brothers are here," Ainsley says, poking her head into my office. She looks frazzled and more beautiful than ever. Since speaking to her uncle on Sunday, she's been more at ease. I think being at odds with him was weighing on her more heavily than even she realized. She's such a gentle lamb.

She cried when she talked to him. It broke my fucking heart to hear her crying so hard. But it was good for her. He told her that he wasn't mad at her. He apologized for making her feel like a prisoner. I don't think he ever realized before she left just how unhappy she was. Knowing her, she didn't tell him. She didn't want to hurt him.

He's coming today to see her. I don't know if she's realized yet that my Brothers are here to support her. I didn't ask them to come. I didn't have to ask. Ainsley is mine, claimed in front of my Brothers in Church and accepted by leadership. Every single one of them will stand at my side and guard her with their lives. We protect what belongs to us.

"Every woman in town will be here to work out if any more of them show up," she says, coming into my office. She circles my desk toward me, her hips swaying. She's got a gym shirt on, my last name stretched across her tits.

I snag her around the waist and pull her into my lap. Surprisingly, she doesn't fight me. She's so shy. When I try to kiss or cuddle her while we're working, she gets all flustered and cute and tries to tell me that we can't make out at work because it's not professional. Like that's going to stop me. I love breaking her rule. She does too.

"They're all here because of Uncle Justice, aren't they?" she asks, laying her head on my shoulder.

"Yeah, lamb."

"I figured."

I don't have to ask how she feels about it. I can hear the smile in her voice. The fact that they all like her seems so surprising to her. It's not surprising to me. She's the sweetest mix of pure innocence and curiosity. She isn't a child, not even close. She's just...Ainsley. The world is a better place because she's in it.

I'm relieved my Brothers are here to support her. I'm guessing Justice Foster knows everything there is to know about me at this point. The fact that he didn't come roaring into town yesterday to drag her away seems promising. But having my Brothers here just in case I'm wrong is comforting.

Our brief conversation on Sunday didn't go great. He was suspicious as hell, thought I was calling for the reward. Like I told him, fuck his money. Don't want it. Don't need it. Some things, some *people*, are priceless. The sweet lamb in my arms is one of those people.

There's not a fucking thing in this world I want more than her. She's been in my life for a little over two weeks, but she's already the best part of it. Without her, the rest seems meaningless. She gives me purpose, completes me in ways I never suspected.

When Knight told me that her uncle was offering that kind of money for her safe return, I was worried as hell. I knew she came from money. But Justice Foster isn't just money. He owns half the state. Politicians curry his favor like he's the Messiah. If shit doesn't go well today, he could make a hell of a lot of trouble for my Brothers.

We're all in agreement that she isn't leaving with him. Down to the last man, they'll fight until the last breath to keep her out of his hands if that's what it takes. But I don't want it to go down that way. For her sake, for their sake...if today doesn't go well, I'll take her and disappear before I let it come to that.

"Are you nervous?" she asks, running her thumb over her bottom lip.

"Nope," I lie. "You?"

"I don't want you guys to fight," she whispers. "I love you both so much. You're my future, but he's been the closest thing to a parent I've had for most of my life. It's going to hurt like hell to lose him if it comes to that."

I don't want that for her, but I can't even lie. It feels good as hell to know she'd choose me over him if it came down to it. I've never wanted or needed much. My bike, my Brothers, and my gym. I need her though. I'd choose her, in this life, in the next one, over everything.

"We're not going to fight, baby gi–" I break off when Patriot appears in the doorway, his expression tense.

"Company," he mutters. "Three SUVs."

Ainsley tenses in my arms.

Shit. Would he bring so many men if he expected today to be easy?

I guess we're going to find out.

"Breathe," I murmur to Ainsley, who hasn't drawn a breath since Patriot appeared.

She sucks in a deep breath and then lets it out, obeying without question. She trembles in my lap, nervous as hell.

I jerk my chin at Patriot, letting him know I heard him.

He steps out, giving us a minute.

I press my lips to Ainsley's temple.

"Everything is going to be okay, baby girl," I whisper against her skin. I won't allow it to be anything less than okay for her. We'll make it through today in one piece. She'll have my ring on her finger, my patch on her body, and my baby in her belly. She'll be in my bed with me tonight and every other night. We'll go on poker runs and to social events with my Brothers. I'll take her up into the mountains and fuck her over the back of my bike on weekends. It's the only acceptable outcome. "I love you and everything is going to be okay."

"Okay, she whispers, pressing her lips to mine. "I love you, Shep."

"I love you too, my lamb." I kiss her gently and then lift her to her feet before climbing to mine. She sticks close to my side, holding my hand tightly enough to hurt. I don't ask her to ease off. Fuck that. She could break every one of my fingers and I wouldn't ask her to let go.

My Brothers are stationed all around the gym. Most aren't even pretending they're working out. They're just chilling, waiting for Justice to get here so we can handle this. Several are packing as if they, like me, worry this could go south in a hurry. They've cleared everyone else out.

Rock, Gage, Knight, Wild, Shotgun, and Rough are stationed near the back of the gym. Blade, Ace, Bear, Hot Rod, Chewy, and Ice have taken up positions near the weight benches. Savage and Bolt are at the front desk with Bullet, who has his boots up on the counter. Rooster and Ranger are standing by the treadmills with Brick and Trigger. Jax, Doc, and Thorn have set up near the front door. Every vantage point in the gym is covered.

"Thank you," I murmur into the room, proud as hell to see every single one of my Brothers here to stand beside me and Ainsley. That sort of loyalty...you can't buy that. Justice Foster can wave his money wherever the fuck he wants. Not a man in this room will bite.

I'm sure the cops across the street wonder what the fuck is going on with every one of us here. I didn't want to do this at the club, didn't want to throw the MC in his face and give him any reason to bring the cops onto the property or endanger the women there. If this goes south, I'd rather shoot up the dirty cop shop than the club.

"We've got you, Brother," Bullet says.

Patriot heads toward the locker rooms, going to cover the back. Slate is out back too. He's not setting foot in this gym so long as Ainsley is here. We may be cool, but I still don't want him near her.

The door of the second SUV lined up behind our bikes pops open. Instead of Justice or his security team, a little blonde jumps out. She's in a sundress and heels. Like Ainsley, she's curvy. Young. I'm guessing this is Milan, the friend Ainsley has told me so much about.

My guess is confirmed a moment later when Justice hops out behind her. I've seen him in the paper several times over the years. He's in his forties, with dark hair and an even darker stare. He's tall and broad, a big son of a bitch. His suit probably cost more than my bike. Even through the glass, I hear him muttering a string of curses.

"No one is going to shoot me on the sidewalk, Justice," Milan says over her shoulder. "I'm going to see Ainsley. If you want your guard dogs to come, tell them to hurry it up."

"That's Milan," Ainsley whispers, relief in her voice.

A couple of my Brothers chuckle at the sight of him following behind her like she's a little queen. Even through the glass, it's obvious he's wrapped around her finger, does whatever she wants him to do. I doubt he'd bring his new wife if he expected trouble, but from the looks of it, she does what she wants to do, his rules be damned.

The door to the gym opens.

"Ainsley!" Milan cries as soon as her green eyes land on my girl.

Ainsley drops my hand and rushes forward. They collide in the middle of the gym in a fierce hug, both talking at once. They cling like they haven't seen each other in years.

I stride forward, taking up a position behind them as Justice steps through the door, two members of his security team flanking him.

Milan didn't hesitate long enough to notice the wall of muscle in the gym. Justice doesn't miss it. He sizes up every single one of my Brothers, clearly not liking his odds. His jaw clenches, his gaze coming to me.

I stand my ground. I'm not afraid of him, his money, or his connections. Hell and I are old friends. I spent more than my fair share of time there when I was overseas. There's not a whole lot I haven't seen or done.

His security guards notice my Brothers. To their credit, they don't even flinch.

"I missed you so much!" Milan cries, squeezing Ainsley as hard as she can.

"I missed you too," Ainsley says, her voice a little softer than Milan's.

"You look so happy," Milan says. Her head comes up, her eyes searching across the gym. Once she catches sight of all my Brothers, she blinks. "Whoa. No wonder you're happy. You're in hot guy heaven here."

My Brothers chuckle again.

"Milan," Justice growls from behind her.

"What? I didn't say I wanted to sleep with them," she huffs, rolling her eyes. "I said they're hot. I have eyes, Justice. I can't make them not work just because you're grumpy."

Justice mutters something that sounds a lot like a threat to spank her ass. Savage, who is standing closest to him hears whatever he says and cracks up. As soon as Milan says Justice's name, Ainsley freezes.

"You two got married," she blurts.

For the first time since getting out of the SUV, Milan falters. Worry fills her eyes. "Please don't hate me," she pleads, tears in her eyes. "I didn't mean to fall in love with him. But he's big and bossy and it's all his fault!"

"Milan," Justice says again.

"It's true!" she cries. "You are bossy."

"He is bossy," Ainsley agrees, flinging her arms around Milan again. "I'm not mad. I wish I had known about you two before all this. Neither of you ever said anything."

"It just happened."

"It did not just fucking happen," Justice growls.

Milan rolls her eyes again, but not before I see the flash of humor in them. I'm guessing he's been trying to get her to give him a chance for a while.

"Hi, Uncle Justice," Ainsley whispers, pulling away from Milan to face her uncle.

I wrap my arms around her from behind, pulling her back against my chest.

Justice looks from her to me, his expression inscrutable. He notices the way Ainsley melts into me, letting me support her. I place my lips against her temple, my hand against her abdomen. He lifts his chin in a silent acknowledgement of my claim on his niece, and then meets her gaze.

For the first time since walking in the door, he actually seems nervous.

"Ainsley," he says.

Milan steps aside, allowing Ainsley to face her uncle.

"I've missed you," Ainsley whispers to him.

"You scared me, kid."

"I'm sorry," she whispers, hanging her head.

My Brothers shift, a ripple of disapproval going through the room. She doesn't owe him an apology. He's the one who left her feeling like she didn't have a choice except to run. She spent a week driving around alone with a million-dollar reward on her head.

Before I can remind him of that, her head comes up, her spine straightening.

"I love you but I'm not going home with you," she says, her voice firm. "I'm nineteen now, an adult. Where I live is my choice."

"I'm getting that," he says dryly.

"Um, this is Shep," she says when I kiss her on the temple again, proud as hell of her for standing up for herself and what she wants. "He's mine."

I fight a grin, fucking loving how she states her claim on me so boldly, as if it's a simple fact of life. I *am* hers. Her name will be my third tattoo, her permanent patch inked into my skin.

My Brothers chuckle in genuine amusement. Milan giggles. Even Justice looks amused at her explanation.

"He's good to me," she whispers.

He glances at me, his eyes hard. "He left out a few pertinent fucking details when we talked."

"I told you what you needed to know," I disagree. "She's where she wants to be and she's safe. With me, she will always be safe. That's all you needed to know."

"And the line of bikes outside?" he growls.

"Every man who rides in that line will keep her safe. And they won't do it by locking her in a cage," I growl right back at him. "She'll never be safer than she is right here. You think your guys kept her safe? They lost her. She drove around for a fucking week by herself before she landed here with me."

Justice grinds his teeth at the reminder that she escaped his people and was out there on her own, defenseless. I'm guessing they had a bad day when he found out. He may be a businessman, but he didn't make his fortune with pats on the back and pep talks. He may be legit now, but we both know his hands have blood on them too. Shit, he's probably spilled more blood and dropped more bodies than half the men standing in this room now.

"They're not bad people," Ainsley says. "They're some of the best men I've ever met. They're good to me and to the people who live here. You're my blood, but they're my family too, Uncle Justice. Don't make me choose between you. I want you to be part of my life."

A murmur goes through the room. Bullet meets my gaze, nodding his head in approval. Several others do too, pleased that she's declaring her allegiance so plainly. That's my lamb though. She's brave as hell when it comes to something she wants. She's been fighting for what she wants since she drove into this town.

The fact that she wants to be here is the only reason Bullet didn't send her back to Justice when Knight told him what was up. He does what's best for the club. In this situation, he easily could have decided to send her back whether I liked it or not. But he has an ol' lady of his own. I think he knows I would have followed mine to hell itself if that's what I had to do. It's no less than he'd do for his.

Justice is less pleased by her announcement than my Brothers are.

"You'd choose them," he says. He seems more resigned than surprised. I don't think he's ever met the woman standing in front of him before now. He's known the sweet little lamb who does what she's told and doesn't make waves. That's not the Ainsley standing her ground now. She's grown since she got here. She's stronger, braver, willing to fight for what she wants. She's willing to fight for me and the club and her life here with us.

"They chose me," she says without hesitation. "I'm here *because* they chose me, and so are they. Every single one of them are standing here now to keep the promise they made to me when Shep claimed me. But I don't want this to become a fight, and I know you don't either. I love you, but I have an actual life here. I have friends and a job and a man who loves me. I can go to the store by myself or go out dancing. I can go on poker runs. For the first time in my life, I'm *happy*, Uncle Justice. Can't that be enough for you?"

He doesn't say anything.

"It's not your fault," she whispers, her voice thick with emotion. "What happened to my parents wasn't your fault. You and my dad made a business decision and something awful happened. That doesn't make it your fault. It doesn't mean something like that will happen to me or to Milan or anyone else you love. You aren't the same man anymore. You have to forgive yourself and let it go."

"Fuck," he curses, striding forward.

Bolt shifts, but a quick shake of Bullet's head settles him.

Justice stops right in front of Ainsley, holding out his arms for her.

She steps forward, flinging herself against his chest.

"You're right," he whispers, speaking so only the four of us standing in our little group can hear him. "I've made us both miserable for too fucking long because I couldn't let it go."

"It wasn't all bad. I had you and Milan," she whispers back. "You gave me everything I could ever want. I just...I'm not like you. I don't want the things you want. When I heard you talking about sending me somewhere safe, I couldn't do it anymore. I should have talked to you about it instead of running."

"You should have," he says. "Because I was talking about sending you to college. But I don't blame you for running. I've been blind for a long time, ignoring what was right in front of my face. I'm not doing that anymore."

"Milan?" Ainsley whispers.

Justice jerks his chin in a nod and then pulls back. He looks around the gym, at each of my Brothers. They hold his gaze, unflinching, waiting for his decision. If blood is spilled here today, it won't be on us.

"If a single fucking hair on her head is harmed, I'll tear this town to the fucking ground. Not a goddamn thing will stop me," he growls, meeting my gaze again. And I know...there isn't going to be blood shed here today. He isn't going to try to take her from me.

"Then we're on the same page," I say simply. Anything happens to her, he won't have to level this town. I'll do it with my bare hands to avenge her.

He holds my gaze for a long moment and then nods.

She's free.

Ainsley practically quivers where she stands as she realizes the same thing. Tears well in her eyes to spill down her cheeks, her expression as bright as the sun. My Brothers relax, the mood shifting as they each work it out for themselves too.

"If she's staying with you," Justice says, "you'll put a ring on her finger. And she won't be one of many. She'll be the only woman in your life, or you'll answer to me."

"She's already the only woman in my life. As for putting a ring on her finger..." I reach into my pocket to pull out the ring box I've had in my desk for the last two weeks. It's over, and she's mine. I'm not waiting another minute to make it official.

"Shep," Ainsley gasps when she sees the ring box.

I drop to my knee in front of her, flipping the box open. The ring is a 2-carat solitaire cushion-cut diamond on a platinum band, elegant and simple at the same time, perfect for my lamb. It was more than worth the price I paid for it. "You're mine, baby girl. You've been mine since you walked through the door at Rooster's. You'll be mine until the day you die. And I'll be yours and only yours," I murmur.

"Property of Ainsley!" one of my Brothers shouts.

The others laugh.

Let them give me all the shit they want. I am her property, bought and paid for by that sweet smile, those bright eyes, and that big heart. No one will ever love her better or fight harder for her. No one will ever cherish her like I do. Not ever.

"Marry me, lamb," I whisper. "Let the whole world know you belong here with me."

"Yes," she sobs, tears streaming down her face. "Yes, Shep."

With my Brothers standing at my side and her uncle and best friend in front of us, I slip my ring onto her finger, putting every piece of my heart into her capable little hands.

Cheers go up around us, loud enough to rattle the windows. I barely hear them. All I hear is my sweet lamb, whispering the sweetest three words I've ever heard.

"Property of Shep," she says, tears still streaming, shining bright as the sun.

I pull her into my arms, right where she belongs. Where she will *always* belong.

And with her lips on mine and her tears dripping onto my face, for the first time in my life...I find my place too. Right here, with her in my arms, my

Brothers at my back, and one hell of a future laid out at my feet.

Chapter Nine

"Where's Ainsley?" I ask Rhonda, poking my head into the classroom. I've been all over the gym since I got back, and I can't find my girl anywhere.

"Haven't seen her," Rhonda says before whipping her head toward one of the high school football players she's been working with for the last few weeks. "Pick up your feet, Darren! Move it!"

I slip out of the classroom, frowning. Ainsley was supposed to meet me here. I had a few things to take care of before we leave for the weekend. We're headed to Cheyenne to see Justice and Milan. They just found out Milan is pregnant. Ainsley's been looking forward to celebrating the good news all week.

Her relationship with Justice has improved considerably in the last three months. He still doesn't trust me much, but for her sake, he tries. I think signing the prenup helped ease his mind. And truth be told, if I were in his shoes, I'm not sure I'd feel any differently than he does. It's obvious he cares about her, even if he did fuck up.

Getting my ring on her finger helped settle me. He couldn't take her from me if he tried. And I don't think he's stupid enough to try. She's made it more than clear that this is where she wants to be. I think he knows this is the best place for her, even if he doesn't like to admit it. She doesn't need to be locked up behind towering walls and escorted everywhere by security. Here, she can go where she wants, do what she wants. She's so fucking happy all the time.

Seeing her happy keeps the same emotion bubbling through me. My life is damn near perfect. I've got my gym, my Brothers, and my wife. I spend every spare moment I've got with her. I can't seem to keep my hands off her. All she has to do is look at me, and I'm hard again, desperate to get inside her and make her wild for me. Learning every inch of her gorgeous body is my favorite thing to do. She certainly doesn't seem to mind it.

She's a dirty little thing when I get my hands on her. She says we're not allowed to make out at work. Breaking that rule on the daily is my new mission in life. I corner her all over the gym just to break it. Her chastisements don't last long once I get my hands on her.

"I'm headed upstairs," I mutter, not really sure which of my Brothers I'm talking to. I don't guess it really matters since a chorus of agreements goes up from the group clustered near the weight benches. They're giving each other hell over something.

I don't stop to find out what. My office is a mess when I pass through it. Half the shit from my desk is in the floor where I put it this morning so I could eat Ainsley for second breakfast before the gym opened. She says I'm greedy, but the hobbits might be on to something. If Ainsley's on the menu, second breakfast is a necessity.

Her shit is all mixed up with mine in the office. I brought her a chair in and made room for her to have her own desk across from mine. Little figurines and pictures are scattered across the top. She rarely ever sits at her desk though. She says that's because I never work when she's in here, which is true. But she likes to be at the front desk, greeting everyone who walks through the doors.

She's enrolled in college. She'll be taking a few online courses in business management this fall. I don't think she's decided just yet what she wants to do with them. She's happy helping me run this place. But she's too smart to settle and I want her to have options. She can do whatever she wants to do. I won't tell her no. She's heard enough of that in her life.

I jog up the stairs to the apartment, grinning when I see the welcome mat in front of the door. I never knew shit like having a welcome mat or seeing her toiletries all over the bathroom could be so fucking peaceful. But there is nothing about it that I don't like.

My apartment feels like a home with her in it. She's always picking up little things, filling our space with personal touches. A few of the ol' ladies threw us a wedding shower after we tied the knot at the courthouse. We have more shit than we know what to do with, but Ainsley always finds a purpose for it. And I'm certainly not going to tell her she can't have something.

As far as I'm concerned, she could paint the place pink and fill it with butterflies, and I'd still be fucking thrilled to have her in my space every day. There's something beautiful about cuddling on the couch after a long day, watching bullshit alien documentaries. Doesn't matter what happens during the day, as long as she's in my arms at the end of it, I'm golden.

"Lamb?" I push the front door closed behind me. Our bags are sitting beside the door, waiting to be loaded into the truck. She wanted to take my bike, but the weather isn't going to cooperate. It's supposed to storm on Sunday. I don't want to be caught out in it on the bike, especially not with her on the back of it. As much as I like to ride, only an idiot tries in a storm.

"In here," she calls, her voice faint, weak.

My hackles instantly go up.

Is she crying?

I take off toward the bedroom, my heart pounding hard. She was fine when I left two hours ago. I'm not even over the threshold before I hear her in the bathroom, dry heaving. My heart sinks into my stomach and then shoots straight up into my throat.

I rush into the bathroom to find her on her knees in front of the toilet. Her face is bright red, her eyes watering. My heart aches at the sight of her looking so miserable. I quickly grab a washcloth and wet it for her before striding toward her.

By the time I've got it on the back of her neck to cool her down, she's stopped dry heaving.

"I don't feel well," she says as if that weren't already obvious.

"Poor lamb," I croon, sinking to the floor behind her and then pulling her into my lap to hold her. "Why didn't you call me? My errands could have waited."

"You can't watch me throw up," she mumbles, slumping weakly against my chest.

"I'm not going anywhere, baby girl." I brush her sweaty hair back from her face. Her skin is flushed but she isn't running a fever. I don't think she's sick at all. I think she's carrying my kid. We've been fucking like rabbits for the last three months. She says her period has never been really regular, but her last one was five or six weeks ago.

"I think I have the plague."

"You sure about that, lamb?" I ask, chuckling at the cute pout that creases her brows and purses her lips. I run my lips across her forehead and then each eyelid. "How long have you been feeling sick?"

"Just today. I was fine until I tried to drink my coffee." She sighs. "I guess we should call Uncle Justice and let him know that we aren't going to make it this weekend."

"I'll call him," I murmur to her.

She hears the smile in my voice and cracks one eye open to look at me. "I thought you were good with going to see them?"

"You aren't going anywhere except back to bed, baby girl." I run my hands down her body, settling one over her stomach. If she's not pregnant, I may actually lose my mind. Three months is long enough. I need her pregnant like I need air.

"I think I should stay here," she mumbles. "I might throw up again."

"I'm not leaving you in the bathroom floor, Ainsley."

"Just bring me pillows and a blanket. I can sleep here."

"Lamb," I say, chuckling. "You aren't sleeping on the floor. I'm going to put you in bed and then I need to run to the pharmacy."

"Don't leave."

The pout in her voice wrecks me a little. Ainsley never asks for anything, never wants anything. She's perfectly content doing the most mundane, boring shit. And I hate telling her no. But she needs to pee on a stick, and we don't have one of those here.

"Come on," I murmur, tightening my grip on her and then rising to my feet.

She clings like she's worried I might drop her, but I will never drop the most precious thing on the planet to me. I've carried her all over the apartment without breaking a sweat. If she's pregnant, carrying her to bed while she carries my kid is the least I can do.

She relaxes once I'm on my feet with her securely tucked in my arms. Her head rests against my shoulder, a soft sigh escaping her lips. We stop long enough for her to brush her teeth. By the time she's done, she's practically asleep on her feet.

I sweep her back up into my arms.

Her eyes flutter closed as I carry her out of the bathroom and then into the bedroom.

Once she's in the bed, I strip her down to her panties and bra and then place the washcloth over her forehead. She grumbles at me that she's fine, but I ignore her. Taking care of her is the best part of my life. I never knew feeding someone, bathing someone, *loving* someone could be so satisfying. But I live for those small intimacies with her.

"I'll be right back," I promise, kissing her on the forehead.

"Okay," she sighs, already dozing off.

I watch her for a long minute, my heart overflowing with love. She is so fucking perfect. I don't know what I did right in my life to deserve her, but I need to figure it out so I can keep doing it. Knowing she's mine and that she might be carrying my kid...my entire life, I wondered what it felt like to be loved unconditionally. Even my wildest imaginings didn't come close to getting this feeling right.

When she sighs my name, my heart rolls over in my chest, lighting up with her name. I quietly slip out of the room and jog downstairs, in a rush to get her a test and get back to her. I need to know now if she's pregnant. Until I do, I won't be able to get a fucking thing done.

"Patriot," I call as soon as I burst out of my office.

He glances up from the weight benches where he's talking to Knight and Bolt.

"Keep an eye on shit for a minute," I tell him, already striding toward the door. "I gotta go to the pharmacy."

"Is Ainsley all right?" Bolt asks.

"She's pregnant."

Matching grins stretch across my Brothers' faces, but I know they come nowhere close to being as big as the one stretched across my own mug.

By the time I make it back to the apartment, Ainsley is awake. She's sitting up in the bed, looking all ruffled and sweet. A crease from the pillow wrinkles her cheek. Her bra strap has slid down, exposing her shoulder. Her face is still pale, but she looks better.

"Hey," she whispers, her voice all scratchy from sleep.

"You feeling better?" I ask, striding toward her.

"Still a little queasy, but I don't think I'm going to throw up anymore."

"Can you pee?"

"Can I pee?" She blinks at me.

I grin, holding the bag out to her.

She eyes me for a minute and then takes it.

"I wasn't sure how many you should take," I murmur. I also didn't know they made so many different kinds. The pharmacist laughed when I dumped about fifteen on the counter and told him to ring me up. He talked me down to four, said they've been flying off the shelves lately and someone else may have need of them too. I'm guessing my Brothers have a lot to do with that.

"Oh my gosh," Ainsley blurts, her mouth opening into a little "o" when she sees what's in the bag. Her eyes fly to mine, a perfect, cloudless blue. "Are you–? Am I–? We're pregnant!"

"Fuck," I rumble, something soft and warm shooting through me as soon as she says the words. I want them to be true so badly I'm willing to do desperate shit to make it happen. "You gotta pee on a stick, lamb."

She bobs her head in another nod, throwing the covers back. Before I can even blink, she's on her feet in front of me, practically quivering with excitement. "I didn't even think," she whispers, tilting her head back to look up at me. "Oh my gosh, Shep. What if we are?" Her hand settles over her belly, making my dick rock hard. And then she freezes. "What if we aren't?"

The little tremor of fear in her voice breaks me. She wants this as badly as I do. But she's had a lifetime of wishing for things that never happened. I think she's a little afraid to let herself hope I'm right. That's all right though. I know deep in my bones that she's carrying my kid. The certainty is just...there.

"Then we keep trying," I say firmly, pulling her into my arms. "But that won't be necessary, baby girl. I already know you're carrying my kid. I knew it as soon as I saw you in the floor."

"I'm scared," she whispers.

"Of being pregnant?"

"Yes. No." She huffs out a breath. "Of taking the test. What if I do it wrong and it says we're not when we really are and it makes us sad? Maybe we should call the doctor and have him do it for me. That way I can't mess it up. I don't want it to be negative, Shep."

"Lamb," I say, trying to soothe her. "All you gotta do is pee on the stick. I don't think there's a right or a wrong way to do that. And I bought extras just in case."

"Okay." She takes a deep breath, settling herself. "Okay."

"Yeah?"

She tips her head back to look at me again. Her eyes scan across my face, her expression softening. "I want to have your babies so bad, Shep. I dream about it sometimes, you know? We're up in the mountains with a little girl who looks just like you. You're carrying her on your shoulders and she's laughing." Her eyes fill with tears. "We're so happy."

"Jesus," I whisper, dipping my head to press my forehead to hers as a current of emotion lances through me. "We're going to have that, Ainsley. What happened to your parents isn't going to happen to us. We're going to have babies and watch them grow up. We're going to have grandbabies and an entire future. Do you trust me?"

"Always," she whispers without hesitation.

I take her lips in a sweet kiss, taste her tears on them. It kills me that she lost her parents so young and in such a traumatic way. Most days, you'd never know what she went through because she is so damn strong. She meets life on her feet, with a smile on her face and joy in her heart. But somedays, especially on the big, important days, that joy is always tinged with a little sadness for her. It's always a little bittersweet.

She misses her parents and the life they never got to live with her. She worries about the same thing happening to us. How could she not when she spent her whole life locked up after losing her parents the way she did?

But the thing she doesn't know, the thing I will always be here to remind her of...is that I'd die a thousand deaths before I let a single hair on her head be harmed. Her life is going to be full and brilliant and beautiful because she's my mission in life now. Loving her, protecting her, cherishing her is what I was born to do. Nothing and no one will ever take me from her or take us from our kids. She may feel vestiges of that sadness throughout our life together, but she will *never* experience that pain again.

"Then trust me when I tell you that you're going to have that, lamb," I whisper, breaking our kiss. I slide my hand down her body, placing it over her stomach. "This little bean will never have to face life without us until she's old and gray and we've lived a thousand lifetimes worth of happiness."

"Little bean," she whispers, and then she smiles. "I like that."

"Yeah?"

She nods, her forehead bumping against mine.

"You ready to go pee on that stick now?"

"Yes," she says, taking a step away from me.

I watch as she shores up her courage, her shoulders going back and a familiar glint lighting her blue eyes. God, I've never seen a sight as beautiful as she is when she's feeling brave. It makes my dick so fucking hard. As soon as she's feeling better, I'll be inside her again. I already know it.

"Um, will you come with me?" she whispers, her cheeks heating. "I know it's probably weird to ask you to watch me pee, but I don't want to do it alone."

"Lamb," I say, shaking my head and chuckling. She's cute as hell when she gets all shy and starts rambling. And I don't care if it is weird. I'll be in that bathroom with her the entire time. "Get your pretty ass in the bathroom. I'm not leaving your side until we know."

"Okay." She hurries toward the bathroom without another word.

Her hands shake when she tries to open the first test. I have to take it from her and open it myself. I'm pretty sure all she has to do is sit and pee, but she reads through the instructions like she's going to be quizzed on them later. I don't rush her though. If memorizing them makes her feel better, I'll wait.

It's hard though. I'm fucking dying to know.

"Oh, it will say pregnant or not pregnant," she says. "That's way better than trying to understand lines and colors and all the stuff Milan had to do." She sets the directions aside and takes a seat. Her eyes meet mine again. "Um, can you turn around?"

"Yeah, baby girl." I hand her the test and then turn around to face the wall, smiling like an idiot. I can't help it. I've been smiling since I made this girl mine. Have a feeling I'll be wearing the same smile for the next seventy years. She is so damn easy to love.

It takes her forever to start peeing, but then it's over quickly.

"Okay," she says after a moment.

I spin around to her flushing the toilet, the pregnancy test in her hand.

"What does it say?"

"We have to wait three minutes before we look," she says, hiding it behind her back when I try to take it from her to look at it.

"Three minutes? What the fuck?"

"It's not that long."

I cock a brow at her.

"Okay, it is that long," she says with a huff, setting the test on a tissue on the counter to wash her hands. "I don't understand why the pee magic can't work faster."

"Pee magic?"

"Yeah, the stuff that works in the test to tell you if you're pregnant or not." She shuts the water off and turns to face me. "It probably has a science-y name, but I don't know what it is, so it's pee magic."

I chuckle, pulling her into my arms. "I love you."

"I love you too," she whispers, pressing her face to my throat.

She's still all soft and warm from her nap. I run my hands all over her body, unable to stop myself. Touching her is addictive. Every part of her is soft and sweet and smooth. There isn't a spot on her body I don't worship.

She slides her hand beneath my shirt, splaying it against my abdomen. My stomach clenches in response to her touch, my body temperature spiking. All it takes is one touch from her, and my dick is hard, begging for attention.

"No teasing," I growl, capturing her hand when she palms my cock through my jeans. "You don't feel well, and I'm not going to fuck you while you're sick, lamb."

"I feel better."

"Good, then you can feel better tucked up in bed with me cuddling you."

She growls at me.

I chuckle, swooping to claim her mouth in a hard kiss. When she starts squirming and whimpering my name, I break away to rest my forehead against hers.

"It's time," I whisper.

She takes a shaky breath and reaches for the test. Her fingers close over it, her eyes squeezed close. "I can't look. You have to look for me."

"Together," I murmur, brushing my lips across her forehead. "Always together, little lamb." I give her a minute to settle and then slowly count to three.

I don't look at the test. When her eyes flutter open, I watch her. I know the minute she sees what I already knew. A little gasp leaves her lips, moisture filling her eyes. Her entire body trembles in my arms, reverence and awe stamped into every line of her face. The test falls from her fingers.

"Shep," she whispers, and then she's bawling.

I scoop her into my arms and carry her to the bed. She clings, her face buried in my throat as sobs wrack her body. I hold her close, crooning to her as joy and love overflow, spilling from my eyes in two drops.

We're pregnant.

Thank you, God.

"I love you so much," Ainsley cries.

"I love you too, my lamb."

"We're pregnant."

I press kisses all over her face, prying her hands away from me so I can kiss down her body. Once I reach her belly, I stop, marveling. My kid is in there, cradled by the most incredible woman I've ever met, protected by the sweetest lamb I've ever known. All of Ainsley's goodness, all of her beauty and grace and sweetness surround our baby.

And I'm the lucky motherfucker who gets to watch them grow.

"Hi, little one," I whisper, pressing my lips to her soft stomach in awe. In joy. In gratitude. "My name is Shep, and I'm your daddy."

Epilogue

<u>Four Years Later</u>

"Faster, daddy! Faster!" Scout squeals, clinging to the handlebars of her little toddler motorcycle. Her blue eyes are bright with happiness, her round cheeks pink. She's in heaven with her daddy pushing her toward the finish line through the impromptu obstacle course the Brothers set up for the race.

Shep and Scout aren't even close to first place, but neither of them cares about that. Scout is just happy to be with her daddy and her cousins. And I know Shep is just happy to be out there with his baby girl and his Brothers.

The Brothers who aren't racing are on the sidelines, cheering on all the kids and taking bets on which Brother is going to make it across the finish line first. Most of the Brothers aren't having an easy time of it. Crouching to push toddler motorcycles across gravel and grass isn't easy! They're being good sports about it though. They couldn't resist when a gaggle of little kids started begging them to race.

And they never do anything halfway around here. If the kids want an obstacle course, the kids get the best damn obstacle course they can put together for them.

The kids are having a blast. I think their daddies are too, even if they are muttering curses and throwing playful insults at their Brothers. They're laughing almost as much as the kids.

I've never met a group of men so in love with their kids. No one messes with the kids without catching hell from the Brothers. Shep is wrapped so tightly around Scout and Raven's little fingers. He can't ever tell his girls no. It doesn't matter what they want, he finds a way to make it happen.

I dread the day Scout asks for a pony. I already know Shep will move heaven and earth to find her one. I love our little farm full of animals not even two miles from the clubhouse, but ponies are a lot of work! With a three-year-old, a two-year-old, another baby on the way, three cows, chickens, and two German Shepherds, I don't have the energy for a pony too!

Shep built me the farmhouse I always dreamed about. It was finished right before Scout was born. I cried when we moved out of the apartment because I have so many good memories there. But every once in a while, Shep and I sneak away during the day to make use of the bed he left upstairs. He likes to wear me out so I nap instead of work. He doesn't know I've caught on to his little plan. I go along with it because it makes him happy. And making him happy means letting him spoil and pamper me. Plus...orgasms are never a bad thing.

Are you kidding me? I love when he gets inside me. He always makes me feel so damn good.

Our sex life has only gotten better over the last four years. He knows my body better than I do, and he worships it. He can make me come in a matter of minutes. It's okay though because I can do the same thing to him. Making him so crazy he begs is one of my favorite things in the world. Nothing is hotter than the way he moans my name, his cinnamon eyes blazing with heat.

I've never felt sexier or more powerful than I do when he's begging me to stop teasing him. My life is magical with Shep and our girls. When I drove into Valor, I never imagined I could have this. But it's been mine every day for the past four years.

Sometimes, things get a little tense when the Brothers are dealing with problems. But I've never felt anything less than perfectly safe. I've never once regretted my decision or missed living with Uncle Justice. There's never been a single day when I didn't love Shep with my whole heart or feel loved by him the same way.

He's the center of my world, the sun around which I revolve. We've spent the last four years on his bike, exploring the world. He never tries to lock me away or keep me from living life. I think he gets as excited for new adventures as I do. He says he loves experiencing the world through my eyes, that it's a lot more beautiful than the world he explored the first time.

I can't wait to have the baby. I'm dying to meet him, and I'm equally as eager to get back on the back of my husband's bike. He doesn't like to let me ride when I'm pregnant. He says my belly gets in the way. I let him get away with it even though I know it's just an excuse. He worries about something happening to me or the baby. It's the only time he ever tries to bubble wrap me.

"We winning, daddy!" Scout squeals when Shep overtakes Knight and Tyler. Tyler, Knight and June's little boy, is the same age as Scout. They play together a lot. "We winning!"

"Yeah, we are, sweet girl," Shep says, and then growls a curse when Knight and Tyler pass him up again.

Scout squeals, demanding her daddy hurry.

I shake my head, smiling.

"Mama."

I glance down to see Raven's blue eyes wide open. She's been sleeping on my lap for the past hour, her little head resting against my belly. She's fascinated that her baby brother is in there. She likes to cuddle with him to nap. It's the sweetest thing.

Her little cheek has a crease on it from my dress.

"Hi, sweetheart," I murmur, pushing her sweaty ringlets back from her face. Like mine, her hair is jet black and curly. "Did you sleep good?"

She blinks her long lashes at me but doesn't say anything. Scout never stops talking, but Raven is quieter, gentler. She loves to stick close to my side, especially when we're around a lot of people. She loves all of her MC uncles and cousins, but she's more content sitting on my lap with her little baby doll than she is playing with the other kids.

Scout squeals again, drawing her attention. She wiggles around until she can sit up on the lounge chair with me. She watches the race for a minute and then looks at me as if waiting for an explanation.

"Daddy and Scout are racing," I say, smiling.

"Oh." She turns back around to watch them. I grab her cup of water off the table beside me and hold it out to her. She takes it and lays back against my stomach, watching the race while she drinks her water.

"She's so sweet," June murmurs from beside me. Like me, she's pregnant. Around here, someone is always pregnant these days.

"Thank you," I say to June, smiling at her. Raven *is* sweet. Shep says she's just like me. Scout is more courageous, braver. She's never met a stranger, and she loves bossing her daddy and her uncles around. They call her Queenie because she's always telling them what to do. They don't mind. They all grin when she gets bossy.

I swear, she's going to be hell on wheels when she's older. It will be all their fault too! They encourage her and her bossy ways. I don't worry about her too much though. With Shep and his Brothers around, I know she'll be just fine.

They're all daddy bears when it comes to the kids. The first time a little boy at daycare made Scout cry, I thought the entire club was going to show up to raise hell. They're the same way with all of the kids. It's so sweet.

Now that I have kids, I understand Uncle Justice a little better. There's nothing I wouldn't do to keep our girls safe, and I know Shep feels the same way. I worry sometimes about what would happen if something happened to me and Shep. It's hard not to think about it sometimes with what I went through. But I don't let my trauma win, and Shep is always quick to remind me that our girls will never lose us that way.

I wish someone had been there to tell Justice the same thing when he took custody of me. He was lost for so long, drowning in guilt because my parents were gone. He blamed himself for their deaths and for the fact that I was there when it happened. He tried so hard to keep me safe, going so far overboard I felt like a prisoner in my own life. I don't think he ever realized how miserable I was. I know that was partly my fault. I should have talked to him. I should have told him. We both made a lot of mistakes.

Our relationship is better now. He's changed so much since he married Milan. She has security, but he tries to dial it back and not go overboard. Milan would kick his ass if he got too crazy. She's good for him. Unlike everyone else, she doesn't just do whatever he says. She's bold and daring, and never takes any crap from him. I think he needed her to upend his life and reshape it.

When he gets too crazy about their kids, she straightens him out. I've never seen Justice as happy as he is with her. He worships the ground she walks on and everyone knows it. No one wants to risk his wrath so they treat her with respect.

We try to visit every few months. Shep and Justice actually get along pretty well now. It was touchy for a while. Neither trusted the other much. But when Milan and I both got pregnant at the same time, they made us both cry. We stormed out and went for ice cream. They straightened up after that. When we visit, they drink beer and shoot pool and give each other crap.

Justice offered to destroy the pre-nup that Shep signed before we got married. Shep refused to let him. He still refuses to let me pay for anything. He says he has plenty of money and we don't need mine. So it stays where it's at, accumulating for our kids. They will never want for anything. Neither will their kids. As for me, I'm happy where I am. I don't need a fancy house or car or any of that stuff. I just need Shep, our babies, and our family.

"You cheating son of a..." Knight growls.

I glance up to see Shep with Scout and her little motorcycle lifted off the ground, hauling butt toward the finish line instead of weaving around the tires set up. The Brothers roar with laughter as he passes the others. Knight picks Tyler up the same way and takes off after Shep and Scout.

Within moments, everyone in the race is doing the same. The kids are squealing and cheering them on. The Brothers on the sidelines are giving them hell. All of the women are laughing too hard to cry foul.

"Daddy!" Raven says when Shep and Scout cross the finish line spray painted into the grass. She drops her cup to stand up in the seat between my legs. I hold onto her as she claps for her daddy and her big sister.

Shep places the bike back on the ground and then scoops Scout up into his arms. She's squealing with laughter, shouting that they won. He kisses her on both cheeks and then sets her on the ground as Knight and Tyler and the rest of the racers make it over the finish line.

The kids are all so excited. I don't think they care who won. They're just happy to have their daddies pushing them around. The Brothers all surround Shep, giving him grief for cheating. He just smirks at them and flips them off when the kids aren't looking.

Scout and the kids run off to play in the grass.

Shep breaks away from the Brothers and heads my way.

"Hey, sleeping beauty," he says to Raven, sweeping her up in his arms to kiss all over her face. His eyes come to me, heating as they run over my body.

I shiver, knowing that look. *Loving* that look. I'll be getting orgasms when we get home tonight. I can't wait.

"You look good riding my cock, lamb," Shep growls, his big hands gripping my hips to work me up and down his cock as I ride him, reverse cowgirl style. His thighs are a mess of scratches. He teased me for an hour before he finally let me come the first time.

My bottom stings from where he spanked me. His marks litter my breasts and inner thighs. He's the perfect mix of hard and soft when we're like this. As soon as the girls are down for the night, he's on me, making love to me until I'm too blissed out to move.

It gets better between us every single time.

"Shep," I moan, throwing my head back and riding him harder. He's so deep like this. I swear I feel him in my soul. I retract my nails from his thighs, sliding my hands up my body to play with my nipples.

"Dirty girl," he growls, lifting me up and then dropping me down on him again. He grinds me against the root of his cock, making sure it rubs across my g-spot. And then I feel his thumb against my back entrance, pressing firmly.

I sob his name so loud I'm surprised the girls don't hear it. He's taken me there so many times over the years I've lost count. I love it every damn time. He's so bossy and demanding, but when he takes my ass, he's so gentle with me. I love both sides of him. I need both sides of him.

I think he knows it because he gives me both now.

"You're so fucking pretty, lamb," he says, working his thumb in and out of my ass as I ride him hard. "Especially when you're on my cock. You live for it, don't you?"

"Yes," I sob. It's true. By the time the girls go down for the night, I'm usually soaked, desperate for him to make love to me again. I try so hard to be quiet for him, but I never can manage it. He soundproofed the room after Scout was born, said if he didn't, the Brothers who live down the road at the club would hear me screaming his name.

He's possessive when it comes to me. Even though I've never even looked twice at another man, he still gets all growly when anyone tries to flirt with me at the gym or even looks at me too long. He's kicked more than a few men out of the gym because he didn't like the way they looked at me. It's completely ridiculous, but there is no reasoning with him.

"I love this sexy ass," he growls, bucking his hips to bounce me on his cock. He's wreaking havoc on my body, unraveling me piece by piece.

"Shep," I gasp, riding him hard. My breasts bounce. My belly jiggles. "God, Shep."

"You going to come on me, baby girl?"

"Yes!" I cry, my inner walls already fluttering around his length.

He bucks his hips again, causing his cock to grind against my g-spot and hit my cervix at the same time. That little lick of pain bursts into a sharp knife of pleasure. I lose my rhythm, lose my mind. My body locks down on him as I come hard, practically convulsing on top of him.

He growls my name and then I'm on my back with him looming over me. His cinnamon eyes are at half-mast, his cheeks flushed. He looks like pure sin as he yanks my ass up onto his thighs and slams inside me again.

I cry out as my orgasm blooms all over again, shattering me into little pieces of bliss and come and love. God, I feel so much love with this incredible man. It's seeped into every pore and vibrates in every cell. And I am so damn greedy because I still want more.

He said once if he kissed me again, he might get addicted to me. I'm addicted too. Once is never enough. I want more, more, more, until we're a sticky, sated heap of tangled limbs and racing hearts and bliss.

"Jesus, Ainsley," he growls, fucking me hard enough to rattle the bedframe. "If I could keep you on my cock, I would. Come for me again. I know you can."

I can't. I *know* I can't...but as soon as he demands it, I go off again, screaming, screaming. This wicked, beautiful man keeps me screaming.

"Ainsley!" he roars, following me over this time. I feel his cock jerking inside of me, his cum warming me from the inside. His body is taut above mine, my name ringing in the room around us. It's heaven, my own personal paradise.

I never knew this type of fairytale life was possible for me. Even when I ran, I had no idea I was running toward a man like Shep and a future like this. I don't know what sent me to Valor, but I know what made me stay. I know what gave me peace. I know who gave me a home.

Shep.

It's always Shep.

"I love you," I whisper, melting into the bed as my orgasm finally recedes.

"I love you, lamb." He leans down, pressing his lips to my nipple and then to my pregnant belly. He gently pulls out of me, making us both groan. I hate when he's no longer inside me. But he never leaves me lonely for long.

He falls onto the bed beside me, his cock still half hard. His arms encircle me, pulling me up against him. I sigh his name, snuggling in with my face buried in his neck and my legs all tangled up with his. He places his lips against my temple and then my cheek, my eyes, and lips. His hand rests against my belly, holding me and his son close.

"My sweet little lamb," he whispers.

"My Shep," I whisper back, and I smile.

With him, I always smile.

Author's Note

If you enjoyed Easy Ride, please consider leaving a review! They are so helpful for authors.

Justice and Milan's story, The Billionaire's Big Bold Wish, is now available. Slate and Constance's story, Easy Surrender, is also now available!

The Billionaire's Big Bold Wish

<u>Excerpt</u>

"Milan," I murmur, closing her door behind me.

"You can't hold me hostage in my own house, Justice," she growls, still pissed. "I want my phone back, and I want you and your men to leave."

"You helped Ainsley run off."

She opens her mouth to deny it and then snaps it closed again. One thing Milan doesn't do is lie. She'd rather have the cold, hard truth than a comforting lie any day. I know that's because she's been lied to and let down for most of her life. She refuses to do the same to anyone else.

"Where'd she go, Milan?" I ask, pacing toward her.

She backs up two steps before she realizes what she's doing. As soon as she does, her chin comes up and she locks her knees. I almost smile at her show of bravery. Almost.

"You know she shouldn't be out there on her own."

"And whose fault is that?" she demands, crossing her arms. She doesn't do it quickly enough to hide how hard her nipples are for me. "You've kept her locked up like a prisoner her entire life. If she shouldn't be out there on her own, it's your fault."

"Where is she?" I push away the flicker of guilt, stamping down on it hard. Ainsley has never been a prisoner. She had everything she could have ever wanted or needed. I may not have let her run wild, but she never went without anything.

Except her parents, whispers that damning little voice in the back of my mind.

Milan shrugs, refusing to answer my question. I don't miss the way she rubs at her wrist though.

Fuck.

"Let me see it," I say, my voice soft. I hold my hand out, waiting for her to obey.

Of course, she doesn't. Anyone else would have jumped to give me what I want. Not Milan. She defies me like always, simply because she knows she can. And like always, that defiance makes my dick rock hard.

"It's fine," she mutters.

"Milan, let me see it."

"I said it's fine."

I quirk a brow.

She huffs out an annoyed breath and holds her arm out. As soon as I wrap my fingers around her hand, an electric jolt shoots straight to my cock.

Her skin is silk. Mine is leather. I may wear expensive suits and have expensive tastes, but I work right alongside my men on the ranches when I visit. It's backbreaking work. Precisely the kind that gives me something to focus on other than the little blonde currently scowling daggers at me.

She squirms as if she feels the same electric charge, pressing her thighs together. She tries to play it off, pretend I don't affect her. We both know she's full of shit. She had feelings for me long before she should have. Hell, she *still* shouldn't. I will never be good enough for her...yet that doesn't change a goddamn thing for either of us. I'm not sure which of us hates that knowledge more. Me? Her? Definitely her.

Loving her may be wrong, but it's the easiest thing I've ever done.

Her wrist is red where the cuffs rubbed against it. It's a superficial injury, but the fact that she was injured at all has my blood boiling. Willis never should have touched her. I don't care if he was simply putting cuffs on her. I don't care if she clawed his eyes out. He should have stood and let it happen. Those are the rules.

You don't touch my niece. You don't touch Milan. Ever.

"Is Willis okay?" she asks, guilt in her voice.

"Don't."

"Don't what?" She blinks her long lashes at me.

"He touched you."

"I punched him in the face," she says, shrugging. "And bit him."

"You bit him?"

"It seemed like a good idea at the time." She bites her plump bottom lip, peeking at me through her lashes. The guilt in those baby blues matches the guilt in her voice. There's a little touch of defiance lurking in them too. "I also kneed him in the balls."

"Jesus Christ," I mutter and then I chuckle. Why am I not surprised she kicked his ass? She's a little firecracker when something sets her off...and nothing pisses her off quite like someone telling her what to do. Obedience means giving up control and giving up control makes her vulnerable. Milan would rather set the world on fire than let anyone see that vulnerability.

We're exactly the same in that regard.

"I'm not telling you where she went," she says, watching me intently. The pulse in her throat flutters, letting me know she isn't as collected as she wants me to believe. She's upset. With me? With Willis? "You can torture me or kill me or whatever it is you plan to do, but I won't tell you."

I stare at her, shocked. Not about her commitment to keeping my niece's secret. I know damn well she means every word. I could lock her in a dungeon and try to torture the truth out of her and she wouldn't say a word beyond fuck off. Her loyalty to my niece is absolute, unshakable. Ainsley means the world to her. She wouldn't betray that bond no matter what. So no, her loyalty doesn't surprise me. It's the fact that she thinks I came here to hurt her.

She could slice me open and pull my organs out one by one and I wouldn't raise a hand against her. She could tear my world apart piece by piece and I wouldn't say a word about it. Neither would my men. My loyalty to *her* is that absolute. I'm not going to hurt her to get my answers.

Never, princess. Not fucking ever.

The Billionaire's Big Bold Wish is now available!

Easy Surrender

EXCERPT

"You're here to ask if you can use my bathroom?" I ask Constance, hoping—praying—she says yes, even though I know damn well she won't.

"No," she says, dashing that tiny sliver of hope all to hell. "Um, can I use your bathroom first, and then I'll explain? I've been waiting for you to get home for a while."

I hesitate for a long moment, my heart sinking into the soles of my boots, and then I roughly clear my throat and nod. "Yeah, owlet," I say quietly. "You can use my bathroom."

I squeeze past her up the steps, gritting my teeth when I brush against her and catch her scent—warm vanilla. Goddamn, she smells edible. My hands shake when I shove my key into the lock, letting her in. I'm not sure if they shake because I want to snatch her up and kiss her so badly or if they shake because her being here now is sure to

ruin my fucking
   month.

Her mother—Jane Nayler—was one of three civilian doctors we were sent to Yemen to rescue in 2019. She was in bad shape with a broken arm and a spreading infection before we ever got to her. By the time we dragged her out of Hajjah, she had a bullet in her side to match. But after killing her coworker, I needed something to do, some fucking way to work
   through the guilt. So I carried her through the fucking mountains to safety while our medic, Luke, fought to keep her alive.

She almost didn't make it.

I shove my duffle out of the way, making room for Constance to enter the house...cabin. I stopped by long enough to drop it inside the front door earlier. I haven't been here in months, but the place is clean and smells fresh, thanks to the service, which comes in twice a month to keep it that way.

"Down the hall," I mutter, pointing the way. "First door on the left."

"Thank you," she says, scurrying past me with her head down.

I watch her ass as she rushes by. I can't help it. It's round, plump, and sexy as hell. And then I shake my head, expelling a heavy breath. Fucking Christ. She's barely nineteen.

If she's here now, I'm guessing it's not because her mom is alive and well. And I made a promise to look after her if anything ever happened to her mom. Back then, I meant it. She was just a sixteen-year-old kid, and I had a debt to pay. But now?

Little Constance Nayler is all grown up.

And I'm thinking maybe I'm just the type of motherfucker she should be protected from. Because goddamn. I want to know what that round, plump ass looks like with my bite marks all over it more than I want my next breath. I doubt that's what her mother had in mind when she exacted that promise from me three years ago though.

In fact, I'm pretty sure I'm the last man she would have chosen to look after her perfect, pristine little daughter if she hadn't been on the verge of death. But it's too late to take it back now. For her and for me.

Easy Surrender is now available!

"You're here to ask if you can use my bathroom?" I ask Constance, hoping—praying—she says yes, even though I know damn well she won't.

"No," she says, dashing that tiny sliver of hope all to hell. "Um, can I use your bathroom first, and then I'll explain? I've been waiting for you to get home for a while."

I hesitate for a long moment, my heart sinking into the soles of my boots, and then I roughly clear my throat and nod.

"Yeah, owlet," I say quietly. "You can use my bathroom."

I squeeze past her up the steps, gritting my teeth when I brush against her and catch her scent—warm vanilla. Goddamn, she smells edible. My hands shake when I shove my key into the lock, letting her in. I'm not sure if they shake because I want to snatch her up and kiss her so badly or if they shake because her being here now is sure to ruin my fucking month.

Her mother—Jane Nayler—was one of three civilian doctors we were sent to Yemen to rescue in 2019. She was in bad shape with a broken arm and a spreading infection before we ever got to her. By the

time we dragged her out of Hajjah, she had a
bullet in her side to match. But
after killing her coworker, I needed something to
do, some fucking way to work
through the guilt. So I carried her through the
fucking mountains to safety
while our medic, Luke, fought to keep her alive.
She almost didn't make it.
I shove my duffle out of the way, making
room for Constance to enter the house...cabin. I
stopped by long enough to drop
it inside the front door earlier. I haven't been here
in months, but the place
is clean and smells fresh, thanks to the service,
which comes in twice a month to
keep it that way.
"Down the hall," I mutter,
pointing the way. "First door on the left."
"Thank you," she says, scurrying
past me with her head down.
I watch her ass as she rushes by. I can't
help it. It's round, plump, and sexy as hell. And
then I shake my head,
expelling a heavy breath. Fucking Christ. She's
barely nineteen.
If she's here now, I'm guessing it's not
because her mom is alive and well. And I made a
promise to look after her if
anything ever happened to her mom. Back then,

I meant it. She was just a
   sixteen-year-old kid, and I had a debt to pay. But
now?

   Little Constance Nayler is all grown up.

   And I'm thinking maybe I'm just the type
   of motherfucker she should be protected
from. Because goddamn. I want to
   know what that round, plump ass looks like with
my bite marks all over it more than
   I want my next breath. I doubt that's what her
mother had in mind when she
   exacted that promise from me three years ago
though.

   In fact, I'm pretty sure I'm the last man
   she would have chosen to look after her perfect,
pristine little daughter if
   she hadn't been on the verge of death. But it's too
late to take it back now.

   For her and for me.

Nichole's Book Beauties

Want to connect with Nichole and other readers? We're building a girl gang! Join Nichole Rose's Book Beauties on Facebook for fun, games, and behind-the-scenes exclusives!

Instalove Book Club

The Instalove Book Club is now in session!

Get the inside scoop from your favorite instalove authors, meet new authors to love, and snag freebies and bonus content from featured authors every month. The Instalove Book Club newsletter goes out once per week!

Join now to get your hands on bonus scenes and brand-new, exclusive content from our first six featured authors.

Join the Club: http://instalovebookclub.com

Follow Nichole

Sign-up for Nichole's mailing list at http://authorn icholerose.com/newsletter to stay up to date on all new releases and for exclusive ARC giveaways from Nichole Rose.

Want to connect with Nichole and other readers? Join Nichole Rose's Book Beauties on Facebook!

bookbub.com/authors/nichole-rose

tiktok.com/@authornicholerose

More By Nichole Rose

<u>Her Alpha Series</u>
Her Alpha Daddy Next Door
Her Alpha Boss Undercover
Her Alpha's Secret Baby
Her Alpha Protector
Her Date with an Alpha
Her Alpha: The Complete Series

<u>Her Bride Series</u>
His Future Bride
His Stolen Bride
His Secret Bride
His Curvy Bride
His Captive Bride
His Blushing Bride
His Bride: The Complete Series

Claimed Series
Possessing Liberty
Teaching Rowan
Claiming Caroline
Kissing Kennedy
Claimed: The Complete Series

Love on the Clock Series
Adore You
Hold You
Keep You
Protect You
Love on the Clock: The Complete Series

The Billionaires' Club
The Billionaire's Big Bold Weakness
The Billionaire's Big Bold Wish
The Billionaire's Big Bold Woman
The Billionaire's Big Bold Wonder

Playing for Keeps
Cutie Pie
Ice Breaker
Ice Prince
Ice Giant (coming soon)

<u>The Second Generation</u>
A Blushing Bride for Christmas

Love Bites
Come Undone
Dripping Pearls

<u>Silver Spoon MC</u>
The Surgeon
The Heir
The Lawyer
The Prodigy
The Bodyguard

<u>Echoes of Forever</u>
His Christmas Miracle
Taken by the Hitman
Wicked Saint

<u>The Ruined Trilogy</u>
Physical Science
Wrecked

Destination Romance
Romancing the Cowboy
Beach House Beauty

Standalone Titles
A Touch of Summer
Black Velvet
His Secret Obsession
Dirty Boy
Naughty Little Elf
Devil's Deceit
A Bride for the Beast (writing with Fern Fraser)

Easy on Me
Easy Ride
Easy Surrender

One Night with You
Falling Hard
Model Behavior
Learning Curve
Angel Kisses

writing with Loni Ree as Loni Nichole

Dillon's Heart
Razor's Flame
Ryker's Reward (coming soon)
Zane's Rebel (coming soon)

About Nichole Rose

Nichole Rose is a short romance author on the west coast. Her books feature headstrong, sassy women and the alpha males who consume them. From grumpy detectives to country boys with attitude to instalove and over-the-top declarations, nothing is off-limits.

Nichole is sure to have a steamy, sweet story just right for everyone. She fully believes the world is ugly enough without trying to fit falling in love into a one-size-fits-all box. When not writing, Nichole enjoys fine wine, cute shoes, and everything supernatural. She is happily married to the love of her life and is a proud mama to the world's most ridiculous fur-babies.

You can learn more about Nichole and her books at authornicholerose.com.

facebook.com/AuthorNicholeRose/

instagram.com/AuthorNicholeRose

twitter.com/AuthNicholeRose

bookbub.com/authors/nichole-rose

tiktok.com/@authornicholerose